THE
Baking Life of
Amelie Day

THE
Baking Life of
Amelie Day

VANESSA CURTIS

STONE ARCH BOOKS
a capstone imprint

The Baking Life of Amelie Day is first published in the United States by
Stone Arch Books
A Capstone Imprint
1710 Roe Crest Drive
North Mankato, Minnesota 56003
www.mycapstone.com

Text copyright © 2014 Vanessa Curtis

First published in 2014 by Curious Fox,
an imprint of Capstone Global Library Limited,
7 Pilgrim Street, London, EC4V 6LB
Registered company number: 6695582
www.curious-fox.com

Library of Congress Cataloging-in-Publication Data
Curtis, Vanessa, author.
The baking life of Amelie Day / by Vanessa Curtis ; illustrations by Jane Eccles.
pages cm
"First published in 2014 by Curious Fox, an imprint of Capstone Global Library Limited."
Includes recipes.

Summary: Thirteen-year-old Amelie Day loves to bake, so she is thrilled to
be invited to compete in the *Best Teen Baker of the Year* contest, and she is
determined not to let her steadily worsening cystic fibrosis get in the way, even
if it means lying to her parents and catching a train to New York on her
own — but when her friend is hit by a van trying to follow her, she is devastated.

ISBN 978-1-4965-2216-0 (library binding) -- ISBN 978-1-62370-506-0 (paper over board) --
ISBN 978-1-4965-2339-6 (ebook pdf) -- ISBN 978-1-62370-590-9 (reflowable epub)
ISBN 978-1-4965-4138-3 (paperback)

1. Cystic fibrosis--Juvenile fiction. 2. Baking--Competitions--Juvenile fiction.
3. Responsibility--Juvenile fiction. 4. Friendship--Juvenile fiction. 5. Families--
Pennsylvania--Juvenile fiction. 6. Pennsylvania--Juvenile fiction. [1. Cystic fibrosis--
Fiction. 2. Baking--Fiction. 3. Family life--Fiction. 4. Pennsylvania--Fiction.] I. Eccles,
Jane, illustrator. II. Title.
PZ7.C948456Bak 2015
823.92--dc23
[Fic]

2014045060

Illustrations by Jane Eccles

Artistic Elements: Shutterstock

Designer: Alison Thiele

Printed and bound in the China
009707F16

To Trevor and Steve,
with love

CHAPTER 1

There was this poem Mom used to read to me when I was six.

Boys were made of slugs, snails, and puppy-dog tails.

Girls were made of sugar, spice, and everything nice.

I probably gave Mom the evil eye when she read that part. I'm famous at school for having an attitude and ranting on about how girls are just as good as boys. I play on the girls' soccer team, and we clobbered the boys just last week, so you can see where I'm coming from.

But that poem must have somehow gotten stuck in my head or gone through my skin and into my body.

If you cut my arm, I bet it wouldn't be blood you'd see pouring out, but pure cane sugar.

If you look into the whites of my eyes, you'll see that they're the tiniest bit yellow. Like the palest, freshest sponge cake made with plenty of free-range eggs.

Even my hair is the color of melted dark chocolate swirling around in a glass bowl that sits over a pan of gently simmering hot water.

I am made of sugar and spice.

I live to bake. My life would be empty without it.

Most of the time there's only one thing on my mind: Flour Power.

***

Mom has gotten used to her kitchen being a complete mess. "If it keeps you happy," she says through tight lips, casting a horrified eye over her stainless steel surfaces, or what's left of them underneath the smears of flour, egg, and butter that mark my residency in the kitchen.

"Mm hmm," I say, but I'm not really listening. Right now, I'm greasing a couple of muffin tins with a buttery paper towel.

"What is it today?" says Mom, checking her lipstick in the mirror and pressing her lips together. Mom works for a lawyer and has to be in full makeup and dressed in a suit by eight each morning.

"Orange polenta muffins," I say, creaming sugar and butter together in Mom's brown ceramic bowl and then pouring flour into a cup on my grandmother's antique scale. The scale is pretty neat. Mom was going to throw it out, but I rescued it and polished it up until it gleamed as dark and shiny as molasses.

"Wow, very twenty-first century," says Mom. "I'm not sure I even know what to do with polenta." She picks up her black purse with the gold chain and takes one last look in the mirror. There's a honk from outside. Mom's friend Yvonne always drives her to work. They share an office and do a whole bunch of boring women's stuff, like splitting bottles of wine over lunch together and going shoe shopping.

"It's a grain," I say. "It soaks up the orange juice and gives the cake a moist texture so that you can add less flour. If you undercook it, you get too much crunch, though."

"Oh, right," says Mom, but she's halfway out the door. I can see Yvonne sitting behind the steering wheel, squirting on gallons of perfume. She's always running slightly late. "Don't forget to go to school, Amelie! And don't forget to take all your stuff, okay?"

I frown.

I'm not likely to forget.

Then she slams the door and clicks off in her heels. I hear the screech of her greeting Yvonne, then another slam and the sound of the car disappearing into the distance.

I wipe my hands on a dish towel and crank up the volume on the radio. Then I glance at the kitchen clock.

Forty minutes until I need to leave for school. Perfect timing.

I pour the juice of four freshly squeezed oranges into my mixture and add the grated orange peel. Then I lift the dripping wooden spoon to my lips and let the raw batter swish around in my mouth.

3

My tongue comes alive with zingy orange and rich, buttery batter.

"Awesome," I say, reaching for a metal spoon. I spoon the mixture into two greased muffin tins and slide them into the oven.

Then I bolt upstairs to get ready for school.

***

I leave a tray of muffins cooling on the rack for Mom to see when she gets home. She works part-time, so she's always home before me. I put the rest in a Tupperware container and shove it into my backpack.

Then I pick up the plumpest one from the rack, dollop a spoonful of rich, creamy Greek yogurt on top, and stuff it into my mouth as I run for the bus. Crumbs and yogurt get all over my clothes, but I don't care. School comes second to baking. I spend the whole day in school dreaming up recipes to try out when I get home.

Even though I'm only thirteen, I recently got a job in the local grocery store. Since I asked to be paid in ingredients, it's okay that I'm younger than the normal hiring age — fourteen. When I asked about the ingredients, Karim, the owner of the shop, looked closely at me over the top of his black glasses and scowled until his hairy eyebrows met in the middle, like two confused beetles.

"You want me to pay you in eggs and flour?" he said. "This is most unusual. Girls your age like to have money for makeup and boys, no? Though I suppose I can't pay you anyway."

His shoulders moved up and down when he laughed. Then he stopped because I wasn't laughing with him. I mean — I do like clothes and makeup and all that stuff as much as the next thirteen-year-old girl, but I'm not obsessed with them like I am with baking.

"Flour, eggs, sugar, and butter, with other ingredients thrown in according to the season," I say in my best business-like voice. "That's the deal. Take it or leave it."

Karim rubbed his brow in astonishment and shook his head.

"You are one crazy American girl," he said. "But okay. I pay you in stuff. Not too much, mind you."

The day I got the job at Karim's shop, I skipped all the way home.

***

School is okay.

In most classes, I sit next to Jenna Smith, my best friend and guinea pig.

She's not actually a guinea pig. What I mean is that I test out all my new recipes on her before I record them in *The Amelie Day Book of Baking*. The book is going to be published one day, and it will be a best seller.

Jenna and I are total opposites, which I guess is why we've been best friends for almost three years. She's tall, blond, and pink-cheeked. She loves clothes, jewelry, and animals. I'm short, dark-haired, and pale, and animals make me cough.

During a passing period, I get out my Tupperware and lean against Jenna's locker as she grabs her books for her next class. I wave the box under her nose until she caves in and takes one of the fat muffins.

"Orangey," she says, sniffing. "Yum. Did you make these today?"

I nod and take another one for myself. "Yeah, of course," I say. "You know me."

Jenna takes a bite and chews on the muffin with a faraway look in her eyes.

"These are the best muffins ever," she says.

I laugh. She says that about every single batch I make. The laugh turns into a cough. Jenna rubs my back.

"Okay?" she says.

I take a deep, steadying breath and nod.

"Polenta," I choke. "That's what gives them their moist texture."

"Mmm," says Jenna. "Could I have another one for lunch?"

I let her take two, and then I eat another one myself, devouring it in three bites.

Most people wouldn't stay as slim as I am if they ate all the cake and calories I chow down every day.

Most people would get fat and pimply and probably die.

6

But then again, as Mom is always reminding me, I am not Most People.

I snap the lid of the box shut.

"Time for French," I say as the bell rings.

I link arms with Jenna, and we head off toward class.

***

At lunchtime I hang out with Harry. I think we're going out. Harry's amazing. He accepts me for who I am. I can't even remember my life without Harry, because I've grown up with him. We've been friends since we were six years old. At one point, his parents lived next door to mine, so he truly was the "boy next door." He's in the grade above me.

And he's a big fan of my baking.

"Awesome," he says, biting into one of my orange muffins with a glint in his dark brown eyes. I bet a lot of other girls wish they were going out with Harry. He's handsome, but not in a preppy, arrogant way — more of an athletic, outdoorsy kind of way.

And he's kind.

"You okay today?" he asks.

I flush a little. I wish people wouldn't keep asking me that. I know it's only because he cares, but it makes me feel like a charity case sometimes.

"Fine," I say. I wave the box of muffins under his nose, and Harry doesn't need much persuading to help himself to another one.

Then I head off to my next class in order to disguise another bout of coughing.

I leave Harry stuffing his face and waving.

***

When I get home, Mom is pacing back and forth by the window.

She's still wearing her black suit, but she's taken off her high, pointy shoes and replaced them with pink slippers, which is sort of an odd look — kind of like two mothers rolled into one.

"This might be it!" she says, waving an envelope in the air just out of my reach and whisking it away every time I try to grab it.

I frown. I'm really tired, and I want to get my homework done quickly so I can invent some more recipes. All day in school I was seeing chocolate sauce and pink mini-marshmallows in my head, and now I want to try out an idea for cupcakes.

"Mother," I say, pulling my long hair back from my hot face, "will you stop being weird and just give me the letter?"

Mom looks at my flushed face, and her teasing smile becomes one of concern.

"You look a little wiped out, sweetheart," she says. "Sit down. I'll get you a drink."

She tosses the letter onto my lap and goes into the kitchen.

I look down at the envelope with my name on it, and my heart does lots of flips and jumps and my chest cramps up.

It's only a letter, I tell myself. *It's not going to bite me.*

And even if it doesn't contain the news I want, it's not like my whole life is going to be ruined . . . is it?

Well — no more than it already has been by other stuff.

I tell myself a lot more comforting and reassuring things, but the other part of me isn't listening.

The other part of me is ambitious and competitive. It is jumping up and down and screaming, "You have to get this, you have to get this!" over and over again.

I pick up the narrow white envelope and slide it open with my fingernail.

I pull out the folded piece of paper and skim it with one eye shut. Like that's going to make any difference.

Then I put my hand to my heart and yell for Mom.

Tangy Orange Polenta Muffins

To make 16 of these orangey little muffins, you will need:

- 2 sticks of unsalted butter
- 1 ¼ cups of granulated sugar
- 4 large eggs
- ¾ cup of polenta (or cooked cornmeal)
- 1 ⅔ cups of plain flour
- 2 teaspoons of baking powder
- The zest and juice of four oranges (save ½ cup juice for the glaze)

For the glaze:

- ½ cup orange juice
- ½ cup granulated sugar

You need to heat the oven to 325°F before you put anything in it. If the butter is hard as ice, put it in the oven in a bowl for a few minutes to soften it up, because there's nothing worse than trying to mix hard butter with sugar — it will make you grumpy and cranky.

You'll also need a muffin tin (or possibly two if you only have 12 holes in each). Grease all 16 of the holes with butter or cooking spray and set aside.

When your butter is melted, cream it together with the sugar. When I say "cream," I mean beat it all together with a wooden spoon. When it's all light and fluffy, then add in one large egg at a time, beating hard in between.

Once that's done, mix in the flour, baking powder, and polenta and then add in the zest (which is the outside of the peel — you can "zest" with a special gadget that your mom or dad probably has in their kitchen, or with a cheese grater) and the juice of the four large oranges (you can either squeeze them to death or use a special juicing gadget, which, again, you might have in a kitchen drawer somewhere). Remember to save ½ a cup of the juice for your glaze later.

By now you probably have one of the gloopiest and most delicious cake batters on the planet — it should be pale orange and tasty. Time to dollop it into the muffin tins using a spoon — fill them almost to the top but not quite. Then put pans on the middle rack of your hot oven and set the timer for about 25 minutes, or keep an eye on them and take them out once they've risen and are all nice and golden on top.

While they're baking, you can make the orange glaze, which is really easy. Just boil ½ a cup of orange juice with ½ a cup of sugar and then let it simmer (on a lower heat) for 5 minutes. Once you've taken your muffins out of the oven and removed them from the tins, stick a spoon in the glaze and drizzle a bunch of it over the top of the muffins.

Allow them to cool down and then serve them with a luscious dollop of homemade whipped cream or plain yogurt, or you could even try adding some ice cream. Hint: they taste even better the next day. Don't ask me why, but they do.

CHAPTER 2

I can't believe it.

"I made it!" I yell over and over. Mom throws her arms around me, and we do an excited victory dance around the living room until we're both out of breath and have to sit back down.

"Let me look at it again," says Mom. She rereads the letter for about the millionth time. "I'm so proud of you, Amelie. You did it!"

I lean my head back against the couch. I feel like I just got punched in the chest and head. It's the relief, after all the months of waiting to get the letter after I sent in my application.

"You should frame that," says Mom. Then she sits down next to me, and we both gaze at the logo at the top of the letter.

America's Best Teen Baker of the Year.

I've made it to the quarterfinals.

That means I have a real shot at world cake domination.

"Hooray," I say in a tired voice. Then I pick up my phone and text Jenna the good news.

Mom kisses the top of my head.

The letter says I have to travel to New York City for the quarterfinals. There's going to be a big competition, based in a trendy glass building designed especially for it, and the whole thing is going to be filmed for a TV show.

I'll be taking part in a bake-off against eleven other teenagers, and the three winners will end up in the semifinals. After that, one person will be eliminated and only two will be left in the final to fight it out for the title of *America's Best Teen Baker of the Year.*

I have to come up with my own recipes for the quarterfinals, and it has to be a mixture of cakes and cookies, too — just to show that I'm not a one-cake pony. I have to do two desserts and one selection of cookies.

I'm a little worried about the cookies. I mean — I *do* know how to make cookies, and they always taste good, but I need something really unique for the competition and, to be honest, I'm more comfortable making cakes. There's something about swirling a spoonful of gloopy white icing across the top of a fragrant little chocolate cake that hits about one hundred on my cake-o-meter.

"I need books," I say to Mom. "Pronto. I mean, I need them like . . . yesterday. Could I have some money?"

"What about your job at the grocery store?" Mom asks. "Or have they stopped paying you?"

I sigh. I've told Mom about a million times that I don't get paid in actual cash. But at this moment, I kind of wish I did. Then I could rush to the bookstore and fill my arms with as many baking books as I could get my hands on.

My brain starts to compute in a wild and furious way, completely at odds with how my exhausted body is feeling.

"I'm broke," I say. "I need money. Please, Mom? Could I have next month's allowance early? And this time could it not go into my savings piggy bank? It's really important."

Mom sighs and reaches for her purse. My heart lifts up, hopeful.

Then she zips it shut. My heart plummets back down into my boots.

"I've got a better idea," she says. "And a cheaper one. Why don't you get onto one of your social networking sites and ask people to submit recipes?"

I roll my eyes and cross my arms. I should've known, though. Except for on very special occasions, Mom always has me put my allowance into this piggy bank on top of my dresser. And she rarely lets me have my allowance early.

I don't want to give Mom the satisfaction of knowing that her idea is actually really awesome, so I skulk off to my bedroom and then dash to my laptop and log on.

I write to all my friends on Facebook, asking them to send me recipes. Then I rewrite my request because I realize that most of my friends aren't quite as obsessed with baking as I am, so I ask them to ask their parents for recipes, too. Then I set up a blog where I can update people with all the news from the competition, and after a bunch of thought, I write my first blog entry and post it. This is what it says:

If you've found this website, it might be because you Googled the word "cake" or the word "bake," or maybe you were just nosing around on the Internet and found me by accident. Anyway, welcome to the first blog post of Amelie Day, wannabe Champion Baker and future author of *The Amelie Day Book of Baking*. I've been chosen as a quarterfinalist in *America's Best Teen Baker of the Year*, and I'll be appearing on a TV near you in the not-too-distant future. I live with my mom, but not my dad. They split up when I was two, but they're still friends — or so they say. Mom is a big fan of my baking, for various reasons that I'm not going to list here because they're boring and I'm sick of talking about them anyway. But all you need to know is that I bake. I love baking. It's my life. Flour Power! Oh, and I need your recipes, especially if you know how to make any really awesome and unusual cookies. So if you have any that you don't mind sharing with me, please post them here.

I stand back and read my first blog post. Then I read it again with my mouth full of chocolate. I keep emergency rations in my backpack and in my desk drawer at home.

Most kids are told not to stuff themselves with junk food all the time, but I'm not Most Kids, and my mom doesn't mind. Besides, my chocolate is really good quality. I rarely buy that gross, sugary, milky stuff that other kids are addicted to, although from time to time it's the only thing that will do when I'm desperate for a quick pick-me-up sugar/calorie fest.

I watched a show about how real, decent chocolate comes from the best quality cacao beans, and I persuaded Karim to order a few bars of the really dark kind for his store, knowing full well that the other customers wouldn't go anywhere near it. He ended up with the bars leftover and unsold — so guess what? He gave them to me as part of my "wages."

I still have some left in my emergency stash drawer. I slide the chocolate out of the pale silver wrapper and enjoy the snapping sound it makes when I break it. I read in a cookbook once that this is a sign of really good chocolate. Then I sniff the rich smell of the beans. It's a sharp smell, a little like lemons. I put one precious square on my tongue and allow it to melt without sucking. It zings into my mouth and seems to wake up my brain. I sit back in my chair with a big sigh and enjoy the sensation. When it's gone, I don't replace it. Sometimes just a little is more delicious than a lot.

I only learned that recently. It kind of goes against everything that Mom is always telling me to do, but I bet the rare day when I don't overeat is probably not going to do me more harm than has already been done.

I log off of my computer and go downstairs to see what Mom is making for dinner.

***

"You'll need some new clothes," Mom says.

We're eating meatloaf with mashed potatoes and peas, sitting at the kitchen table together with the old French doors thrown open to the courtyard outside. Our house used to be part of an old stable for a colonial estate. The mansion has long since gone, but the stables and carriage houses were converted into homes years ago. We live on the very end of the block. Next to our house is a huge arch where the horses and carriages used to pass through, but nowadays cars drive through it to park outside their houses instead. If you look closely up at the arch you can still see hinges where the grand gates once were, and our house is full of beams with old nails hammered into them for holding horse tack and harnesses. It's what Mom calls a "house with character" when she's describing it to people she doesn't know. It's drafty in winter, has low ceilings and tons of creaky floorboards, but the great thing is that it has an enormous kitchen that was once made up of three rooms, but had the walls knocked down. There's a cooking station in the middle with stools around the outside where we eat meals, or in my case, do homework or bake myself into oblivion.

Mom got the house when she and Dad got divorced. Dad came from a rich family, so he was generous when they split up and even went house hunting with her until she laid eyes upon the run-down converted stable where we now live. He paid extra to have it renovated, and we've been here in West Clinton, Pennsylvania, for eleven years.

I love our house, but most of all I love the kitchen. That's where my heart belongs. That's where I truly feel at home.

"I don't need any more clothes, Mom," I say.

My mind isn't on clothes tonight. Or any night, come to think of it.

I just logged on to my blog, and already there are two recipes posted by complete strangers. One of them, from a girl named Jane, is for chocolate chip and peanut butter cookies. My eyes light up, and I print off her recipe. I'm trying to read it now, but Mom keeps interrupting me.

"Yes, but don't you want to look nice on TV?" asks Mom. She glances at my purple leggings and white T-shirt with a giant picture of a purple cupcake in the middle of it. "You look beautiful when you make the effort, Amelie."

She comes over to where I'm sitting, pushing my peas around while I scan the recipe, and pulls my hair back onto the nape of my neck.

"I wish you'd wear your hair up in a nice bun instead of in this bird's nest," she says, releasing it back into its usual scruffy position. "You have a great profile. Like an actress or something."

I bat her away with my hands. "Mom," I say. "I'm so not in the mood. It's more important that I actually know what I'm going to cook for this competition, isn't it?"

Mom sighs and loads the empty plates into the dishwasher.

"Well, I'm going to take you shopping this weekend," she says. "No arguing. I got paid a little bonus last week, and I think we both deserve a treat."

"Okay, okay," I say. "Whatever. And now I need to go and experiment with peanut butter, if that's all right with you."

Mom turns around with a plate in her hand.

"Amelie," she says. "We need to talk about how we're actually going to manage the trip to New York. I mean — it's going to be tough on you."

I'm about to say something rude, because I hate it when she makes a fuss. But I guess I know that it comes from years of caring for me and worrying about me, so I bite my tongue and go over to the kitchen cupboard I've labeled AMELIE'S STUFF.

I stare at all the beautiful rows of cans and jars and bottles and packets, but my eyes seem to have misted over or gotten tired or something, because for a moment I can't see.

Then the mist clears.

I grab a jar of peanut butter and twist the lid off.

I spend the rest of the evening trying not to think about what Mom just said.

CHAPTER 3

We hit the mall on Saturday. Jenna, whom I brought along for moral support, is with us. Mom tends to get a little carried away when confronted with the joy of dresses and shoes. Granted, Jenna loves that sort of thing too, so I'm not expecting much help from her either.

Mom heads into the very first clothing store that we come across.

"I don't even *like* their stuff," I groan, but Mom has developed her usual selective deafness and is already throwing dresses over her arm and rifling through racks and shelves with a determined frown on her face.

"This would be a lovely color on you, Jenna," she says, holding up a pale yellow strappy dress in thin cotton against Jenna's pink skin and blond hair. "It wouldn't suit Amelie, though. She needs bolder color against her dark hair."

"Actually, Mrs. Day, I really love that," says Jenna, spinning around and holding the dress up against her in front of the mirror. "But Mom hasn't given me my allowance yet, so . . ."

She makes a sad face and hangs the dress back on the rack. Jenna knows how to play my mother like a deck of cards. She comes from a single-parent family, just like me. Her mother has a part-time job at a supermarket, and there isn't much money left for new clothes. Jenna and her mom come over for Christmas dinner every year so that Mom can make a big deal about them being there and show off her huge kitchen and my baking skills at the same time.

Jenna is successful, as usual.

"Oh, Jenna," says Mom, putting an arm around my best friend. "If you love it, then you shall have it! I got a bonus last week."

She gives Jenna some money and gestures at her to go pay for the dress. I swear that my friend actually *skips* up to the cash register.

I shudder and give Mom my disapproving look, but I can't help smiling. She's a cool mom, most of the time.

When she's not worrying about me, that is.

"And what about a dress for you?" Mom says. "Come on! You might make it to the finals — you never know! Then there will be millions of people watching your every move on television."

When she says this, I get butterflies in my stomach. That makes me think about butterfly buns, a recipe I just tried for the first time a week ago. The buns are made so they look like they have little wings sticking out, with cherry preserves and whipped cream in the center for the butterfly's body. I'm so wrapped up in thinking about whether or not I could use blueberry preserves instead that I don't even notice, really, when Mom shoves an armful of dresses at me and pushes me into a fitting room.

The dresses are all ugly. I hate dresses anyway. Although I have long dark hair and a girly sort of face, I'm not really into dressing in cute clothes. I like leggings, jeans, boots, and T-shirts, and I like leather jackets best of all.

In the end, I reach a compromise with Mom. I agree on a sleeveless tunic with a gray and white pattern on it, some cropped black leggings, and a pair of black ballet flats. It all kind of goes with my hair and complexion, so she's happy enough, and I can't wait to get out of the store and go home.

I'm starting to feel kind of weird.

I glance in the mirror as we leave the shop with our bags. My skin has a grayish-blue sort of tinge to it. I try to walk ahead of Mom so she doesn't notice, but Mom is trained in the art of monitoring my health at all times, and she has some sort of psychic radar that now causes her to catch up to me and stare me straight in the eyes.

"You don't look too good," she says, dropping her bags and putting both hands on my shoulders. "You can't be getting another infection, can you? You're on so many antibiotics already!"

My head starts to swim, and my chest tightens up.

"Uh-oh," says Jenna, who knows the signs almost as well as Mom does. "Should I get somebody?"

Mom ushers me back into the store and pushes me into a chair. A concerned employee hovers behind her. There seems to be a crowd gathering. Wow. I must look really bad.

"Inhaler," I choke. My mom reaches into her huge purse, pulls out a small plastic blue device, and passes it to me. I take several deep puffs, but it's not enough to stop the cough from coming.

I double over and cough like I'm trying to cough my heart out of my body. Sometimes it feels like I might actually succeed. That would be gross. Imagine coughing your heart out of your mouth. Ew.

"Take it easy," Mom says. She's crouching down in front of me now. Her tan has faded, and her face looks all papery and old. "Jenna, could you get the water out of my purse?"

Jenna passes over the water bottle with a solemn look. Her new yellow dress lies forgotten in its bag on the floor.

I gulp some water and cough some more and then at last the choked-up feeling in my chest subsides a little as the inhaler kicks in and does its work.

"Wow," I say, wiping my eyes. "I felt fine when we got here."

"Hmm," says my mother, pushing my hair back from my face. "I'm really not sure we should even be thinking about going to New York for this competition, Amelie. A week in New York City — with the pollution and everything in the middle of summer — it's a crazy idea. I think I'm going to have to go back on what I said. We can't go to New York, and that's that."

My eyes are watering again as we walk out of the store in silence. This time it's not the coughing that has made my eyes tear up, but the sinking feelings of gloom and disappointment that are threatening to engulf me.

Mom opens the car door in silence. Jenna slides in next to me in the backseat and gives me sympathetic looks, but she doesn't dare speak. She fingers the plastic bag that holds her dress. I can tell that she's dying to look inside but doesn't want to appear selfish.

I spend the journey home with my head buried in my hands.

I hate this stupid illness and what it does to my life.

Oh. I didn't explain, did I? What's wrong with me, I mean.

I suffer from an illness called cystic fibrosis.

There is currently no cure for it.

This basically means I'm going to die.

CHAPTER 4

When I say I'm going to die, I don't mean right away.

Lots of people with cystic fibrosis now live into adulthood. I met somebody at the hospital who was almost forty, and to me that seemed pretty ancient, so I was impressed.

I've had the illness since I was born. You get it if both your parents carry a faulty gene, and it looks like mine did. I know that Mom still blames herself whenever I get sicker, which is stupid, really, because I don't blame her, and how could she have known she carried the faulty gene? I got diagnosed before my first birthday after Mom noticed that whenever she kissed me, she could taste salt. People with CF produce more salt when they sweat. So they gave me the sweat test and told Mom that I had the illness.

Having cystic fibrosis means that there are two big problems I have to live with on a daily basis. The first is that my lungs fill up with mucus, and I feel like I'm going to choke. I have ways of treating this at home or in the hospital, but it takes up huge chunks of time and that's a real pain. The other frustrating thing is that my digestive system doesn't work as well as it should, and I have trouble digesting my food. I have to take special pills called enzymes with every single meal I eat — otherwise I get a horrible stomachache and might throw up.

There are upsides to having cystic fibrosis, though. I'm allowed to stuff my face! So for lunch I can have grilled cheese sandwiches and potato chips and thick chocolate milk shakes, and that's just for starters. I snack throughout the day on chips and cookies, and the teachers make an exception for me because they know that if I don't eat enough, I'll keel over and then my mother will come rampaging down to the school and give them a piece of her mind.

The weird thing is that even though I eat tons of junk food, I'm underweight and my skin is clear and glowing. Jenna gets really annoyed about that. She eats salad for lunch every day and gulps down all-natural juice, but she has a ton of pimples.

"I don't get it," she says. "You practically *live* off of cake. Why is your complexion so good?"

I smile and look superior whenever she says this. With cystic fibrosis, you have to take all the compliments you can, whenever you can get them.

I struggle to keep looking good. It's one of the things about CF that I really hate. Yeah, I can eat whatever I want, whenever I want, but the downside is that despite all of that, I'm still really underweight and bony. I'm also pretty short, since CF prevents you from growing to the same height as everybody else.

Jenna thinks I'm pretty, though.

"Your hair is to die for," she said once. Unfortunate choice of words, but I laughed anyway. My hair is so dark it's almost black and very long and shiny. "And you've got a heart-shaped face."

It's true. I do have an okay sort of face. It's just my body that lets me down.

For all the things going wrong inside of me, I take pills. Hundreds and hundreds of them. Some of my medicine is inhaled from a nebulizer, but a lot more of it comes in the form of pills.

Every morning, Mom hands me a pillbox with the days of the week written on little plastic compartments, and I open my mouth and gulp down a handful of pills with a glass of water. This is what I take:

Pills to open up my airways.

Pills to stop my stomach acid from coming up and burning my throat.

Multivitamins to keep my general health levels as high as possible.

Pills to help my body break down fats.

Pills to help me breathe easier through my sinuses.

Vitamin K for bone strength.

Antibiotics to stop chest infections.

I take all of these more than once a day. Mom counted them up once and told me that I take seventy-five pills every single day.

So.

As luck would have it, my growing up with cystic fibrosis started to coincide with my love of baking, and since I need to consume at least three thousand calories each day, it seems like the perfect career to be aiming for. Even Mom can't really argue with that. I think she secretly wanted me to be something like an accountant and earn tons of money, but now that I'm on the path to achieving world cake domination, she's wise enough to see that she can't really stop me.

Nothing and nobody can get in the way of my ambition now.

I'm determined to get to New York, whatever Mom says.

I'm going to bake my way to the top.

Flour Power!

***

You might think that people with cystic fibrosis can't have real relationships. You'd be wrong.

Harry's really cool about the whole thing. I've had it the whole time I've known him, which is basically forever. But when we started going out, I reminded him that life with a CF patient isn't exactly fun.

"I hang out at hospitals a lot," I said. "If you're looking for a bouncy person with lots of breath, you'd be better off asking Jenna out instead."

There. I gave him every chance to back off and run away in horror from the crazy sick girl with the backpack full of cake and the ribcage that poked through her T-shirt.

Instead he reached out and took my hand.

I was so surprised that I lost the power of speech.

Not for long, though.

"Did you hear what I said?" I asked. "I'm not always a lot of fun."

Harry continued to hold my hand and stare into my eyes. Inside my chest there were little flutterings and leaps, and for once it had nothing to do with excess mucus production or the beginnings of some nasty infection.

"So?" he said. "We've all got to die sometime, right? Any of us could die tomorrow. It's no big deal."

I continued to stare at him in amazement. I thought that most boys wouldn't want a girlfriend who spends most of her free time coughing, puking, fainting, being hooked up to an antibiotic drip, or puffing on an inhaler, but then again, Harry seems to not be like Most Boys, in the same way that I am not like Most Girls.

"Besides," he said, "you make awesome cakes. And I kind of like to eat a lot of cake. So I think we probably should go out sometime."

I looked into his dark eyes and at his brown floppy hair, and from that moment on I've been smitten.

"I will be your cake tester," he said as he left. "You can try out all your recipes on me."

That did it for me. We've been together ever since.

***

I'm sitting in the local park with Harry and a big wicker basket that I stole from Mom.

It's a beautiful day. Kids are playing on the swings, and mothers are standing around in little huddles gossiping or eating ice-cream cones.

I'm feeling a little down, even though it's great being with Harry on a Sunday with the sun beaming and the whole day ahead of us.

Mom isn't budging on the whole New York thing. She took me to the doctor the day after I collapsed in the clothing store, and he said that it might be that my lung function has decreased. I won't know for sure until my annual checkup, but Mom has been tasked with forcing me to rest, take extra medication, and have early bedtimes.

That means that I've had to stop playing on the soccer team at school, at least for a while. It's a pain, because when you have cystic fibrosis, it's really important to exercise a ton to keep your lungs working as well as they can, but lately I'm getting too out of breath to run on the field. It also means that I haven't been studying for my tests as much. I still do all my homework, but I have to go to bed earlier or else Mom starts yelling swear words up the stairs.

Mom is very fond of Harry. I heard her whispering to him about my current state of health as we left the house, but I pretended not to notice. It's kind of embarrassing. Harry can see how healthy I am just by looking at me, so there's no need for Mom to be all anxious and over-motherly, but I'll probably never be able to stop her.

"Pig in a blanket?" I ask, offering Harry the first of about twenty plastic boxes from Mom's picnic basket.

Harry's eyes light up. He's not at all overweight or anything, but he does love food. Most of it gets burned off during football practice or biking. Harry is very into his sports.

"Made by you?" he says. "Stupid question. Of course they're made by you."

He sinks his teeth into the warm, greasy pastry and closes his eyes for a moment.

"Awesome," he says. "Best I've ever had."

I kind of know he's not lying, either. I've perfected my pigs in blankets over the last year by using top-quality flour and organic mini pork hot dogs I buy from the butcher at the local farm stand with my allowance from Mom. I'm pretty confident that I've achieved just the right balance between moist, savory meat and crisp, flaky pastry. I've brought two little jars of a mustard dipping sauce I made. Harry spoons the sauce all over another pig in a blanket and bites into it with his usual enthusiasm.

I'm less hungry today. My chest is tight, and the stronger antibiotics that the doctor put me on to avoid another chest infection make me feel a little sick. I pass on the pigs in blankets and search through the picnic basket for cake instead. Somehow it's always easier to eat sweet stuff when I'm feeling sick.

I open the lid and peer inside. Four perfect chocolate cupcakes nestle up like newborn kittens in a box, waiting to be chosen. The chocolate frosting glistens in the sun.

I pick out the special one I made for Harry and pass it to him.

"Aw," he says. "That's sweet. Thanks, Mel."

Harry always calls me Mel. He thinks Amelie isn't really a name that fits me, and he might be right. He also says it reminds him of a really long, dull French film that his mother forced him to watch once.

"It was all doors swinging back and forth in slow motion," he said. "Borrrring."

He's picking the tiny red heart off the top of his cupcake and popping it into his mouth. I had the heart idea this morning when I looked in my special cupboard and found a forgotten roll of fondant icing. Fondant is kind of cheating and I prefer to make my own, but it's good for coloring and making into shapes, so that's what I did.

I made Mom one of the special heart cupcakes as well and left it in the kitchen for her to find. Even though we're kind of not speaking over all this New York stress, I still think that she deserves a cupcake.

Mom has gone through a lot over the last thirteen years.

I suppose it can't be easy having a child with my illness to look after, even though I'm not really going to be a child for much longer.

It's why she and Dad stayed on good terms, too. They decided that it wouldn't do me any good to live between two warring, battle-scarred, and bitter parents, so they made a pact to stay friends for my sake, and they've pretty much managed it ever since.

"Could I have another one?" Harry asks. He's gazing into the cupcake box. "These are my favorite, definitely."

I smile and pass it over. Then I force down another one myself. Got to keep the calories going in. If I keep eating and get stronger again, maybe Mom will let me go to New York for the competition.

"I hope so," says Harry. I didn't realize I'd spoken my last sentence out loud. "I know how much you want to go. I'll go with you, if you want."

I smile and let him take my hand, but my eyes are focused on the dark gray storm cloud threatening to pass over the sun and ruin our lazy picnic.

I don't feel so good today.

What if my lung function goes downhill?

What if I end up in the hospital again instead of taking part in the competition?

I shudder. Sometimes having cystic fibrosis seems a little like someone's playing a bad joke on me.

Most of the time I try to stay positive. Mom has always made a big deal out of telling me that I'm special and asking me, "Who wants to be like everybody else anyway?

"You're unique," she says. "And you have unique and creative talents, too."

Yeah. But there's not much point having the talents if I can't do anything with them, is there?

For the first time in a long time, I wish that I were normal.

Like Jenna, like Harry.

Just like everybody else.

Best-Ever
Pigs in Blankets

To make 20 of these delectable mouthfuls, you will need:

- 1 8-ounce can of crescent roll dough
- ¼ cup Dijon mustard
- 20 mini hot dogs
- 1 egg
- Poppy or sesame seeds

To make a dipping sauce for these lovely bites you will need:

- ½ cup sour cream
- ½ cup mayonnaise
- 3 tablespoons Dijon mustard
- 1 tablespoon ground mustard

Preheat the oven to 350°F. Take out your crescent roll dough and cut each triangle of dough into thirds, lengthwise. Brush the strips of dough with Dijon mustard.

Now for the fun part! Put the mini hot dogs on one end of each strip of crescent roll dough and roll them up.

In a small mixing bowl, lightly beat one egg. Then brush the egg wash onto the top of the pigs in blankets to make them nice and shiny in the oven. Put them in the oven for about 12–15 minutes.

While they're baking in the oven, you can mix together the tangy mustard dipping sauce. Just mix the sour cream, mayonnaise, Dijon mustard, and ground mustard together in a small mixing bowl and — presto! You've got an extra-delicious addition for your pigs in blankets.

Take them out of the oven when they are all puffed up, sizzling, and golden brown. Serve the first batch of them hot with the dipping sauce on the side. You will be in heaven.

(Note: my mother steals these during the night when she's hungry. You might want to invest in a lockable container.)

CHAPTER 5

I take two days off from school because I've been feeling really awful.

Mom isn't too impressed when I drag myself into Karim's shop to do two afternoon shifts, but the thing is, I need the ingredients to be practicing for the competition in New York.

"Oh, goodness me," says Karim as I lean on a shelf full of bread to catch my breath after a coughing fit. "Little baking girl doesn't sound too good today. Maybe you should take break."

I stand up straight and continue stocking shelves.

"Little baking girl is fine," I say, even though one look at my reflection confirms that I'm really not. My face is all white and strained-looking, and my lips look slightly blue. This lack of oxygen thing is a real nightmare at times. At the tiniest physical exertion, I find myself having to sit down and rest like a sad old lady.

The hospital gave Mom an oxygen tank, which I plug in at bedtime. It means that I have to put plastic tubes in my nostrils, and then the oxygen gets into my body and makes me feel a little better by morning. The last thing I want is to have to travel around attached to it, but Mom found out that there's a smaller version of the tank that I could carry.

When it's bad, cystic fibrosis can be *really* bad. Some days I struggle to take a real breath and even to climb the stairs. When it's good, I can almost convince myself that there's nothing wrong with me at all.

Almost.

Karim watches me with concern all afternoon. He's got my mother's cell phone on speed dial, which is really embarrassing, but she insisted on it as a condition of me being allowed to work.

"I think you should finish early," he says. "I will still pay you the same. Okay?"

I know when I've been beat. I can hardly stand up straight, and all I can think about is getting home and lying on the couch with a bucket and an inhaler. I take a few sneaky puffs on it now, with my back to Karim. The drugs loosen the tightness in my airways a little, and I sigh with relief. One more big cough, and I feel slightly better.

"Okay," I say to Karim. "Thanks. Could I take butter and eggs and white flour today?"

Karim gestures at the shelves of his shop, arms out wide.

"Take whatever you want, little baking girl," he says.

I bet he still saves money by not paying me an actual wage, so I don't feel too guilty about loading up my bag with several boxes of butter. I also take some free-range eggs and flour. I'm planning to buy cheese at the special cheese shop in town. Karim does sell cheese, but it's hard, square, in packets, and tends to be American. I'm looking for something a little more special, like a nice sharp cheddar, so that I can cook up a fattening batch of cheese straws to put in my school lunch box for the next few days.

That's if I ever go back to school.

The doctors are threatening to keep me in the hospital for tests and observation unless my lung function stabilizes over the next few days, and Mom is in full agreement with them.

There's less than a month until the *Best Teen Baker of the Year* competition.

And there's something else on the horizon.

It's something I try not to think about, but every time my lungs get worse, it takes a sneaky step closer and looks over my shoulder.

If things don't get better, I'm going to have to have a major operation to save my life. It's called a double lung transplant. It means that I would have somebody else's lungs put into my body and my own diseased ones removed.

Gross.

***

When I get home, I lie on the couch and turn the TV on, but I can't concentrate. There's nothing but cooking shows on, and although usually I love watching other people cook and come up with ideas, today I just feel resentful that I'm not in the kitchen whipping up my own recipes.

The thought of standing at the stove makes me feel exhausted. I stay on the couch for the rest of the evening. I can't face climbing upstairs to bed, so Mom brings over a blanket and puts it on top of me instead, but even then I can't sleep.

I lie awake watching the moon outside and devising new recipes in my head. Then I just lie there, thinking about my life and where it's going — or not going.

Sometimes people at school ask me what it's like living with an illness that's never going to get any better. I don't mind them asking, because I think that they truly want to know the answer. It's hard for somebody who is well and has a healthy digestive system and strong, pumping lungs to understand what it's like to not have those things right from the very start of life.

I tell them that I feel the same things as everybody else — happiness, sadness, pain (although maybe more of that than your average kid), excitement, boredom, hunger (on a good day). On a day-to-day basis, I guess I pretty much feel the same things in the same way as any other teenager.

"But what's it like not knowing if you're going to reach adulthood?" some people ask. "What about making plans and stuff? And college."

I look them in the eye.

"Most of the kids my age don't have a clue what they want to do when they graduate," I say. "And actually, I do know. I want to bake."

I can see by their doubtful expressions that they don't believe this, but I need to sound strong and positive about everything, or else I'd curl up under my blanket and never come out again.

I sigh and sit up. It's obviously going to be one of those nights where thoughts whirl around in my head and keep me from sleeping.

The thought of whirling makes me think of cinnamon whirl cookies. I scribble a few ideas down on a pad of paper. I could do strawberry jam-filled whirls, I think. Made with really good flour and country butter, homemade jam from my cupboard, and dusted with powdered sugar. Or maybe I'll experiment with chocolate whirls instead, sandwiched together with smooth, sweet chocolate buttercream and dipped in hot dark melting chocolate so that half of the cookie sandwich is plain and half dipped.

Then I remember my blog. I reach under the couch and slide out my laptop to log on.

There are six more replies to my first post! Five of them are from people offering cookie recipes. The sixth is from some girl wishing me good luck with the competition.

I scan the recipes, and my mind starts to buzz with chocolate chips and vanilla extract and big, luscious chunks of fudge.

I feel inspired, so I click on the menu bar on my blog and select "new post." Then I tuck my legs up under my blanket and balance the laptop on my knees.

This is what I write:

Hi, it's Amelie here — the girl who bakes.

Wow, I'm really amazed to come on and find all these delicious cookie recipes. I promise I will try them all out when I have the time and energy. That's not supposed to sound pathetic. The thing is, I kind of suffer from an illness, and it saps a lot of my strength. That's why I bake — because I am supposed to try to fatten myself up as much as possible in order to stay alive. Plus I just love baking — it's my favorite thing in life, other than Harry (my boyfriend) and my BFF, Jenna.

Anyway, you know how last time I wrote about that competition in New York? The one I made the quarterfinals for? The thing is — I'm too sick to go. Or at least my Mom thinks I am. So now I'm not just drowning in mucus (sorry, TMI!), but also in disappointment.

But anyway, please keep sending me your recipes. Any good, sticky cake recipes with a twist would be great. Have any of you ever tried making chocolate lava cake? If not, go look it up and try to make it. Post a photo online if you can. It's kind of a challenge to get the middle part runny and not too firm. I'm signing off now, but I'll post an update of what's happening in my ever-changing life soon.

For the first time all week, I feel the prick of something resembling an appetite. I lurch up off the couch and stagger into the kitchen.

The clank of pans and me banging into cupboards brings Mom downstairs all prepared to be cranky, but when she sees me stirring a frying pan of rich scrambled eggs and cooking up crispy bacon to sprinkle over the top, she grabs a plate and sits down.

"It has been forever since I've had a midnight snack," Mom says. "It will go straight to my hips, but who cares?"

She's grinning. I can tell she's relieved that I'm starting to want to eat savory stuff again. It's usually a good sign.

"Mom?" I say, spooning the creamy eggs onto her plate and sprinkling the salty shreds of bacon on top. I grind black pepper onto my eggs before I add the bacon. I serve the bacon and eggs with soft, homemade whole-wheat bread with tons of butter. Then I put a strong pot of tea in the middle of the table and pour milk into two cups. "If I get better this week, could we talk about New York again?"

Mom puts down her fork. "Amelie," she says, "I've discussed this with your father. We really don't think that any time spent in the city is going to be good for your health, and your health is our priority."

I make a sulky face before shoveling forkfuls of bright-yellow egg into my mouth. The free-range ones are always this sunshine-yellow color, like the chickens have spent many happy hours pecking about in sunlit grass. The bacon is a great contrast — sharp, salty, and with a nice fatty aftertaste. Dad says that my breakfasts are the best in the world, and I think he might be right.

"Can't we see how I am in a couple of weeks and make a decision then?" I plead, pouring Mom a steaming-hot cup of tea. "We don't have to decide right now, do we?"

Mom scrunches her lips together.

I know she finds it really hard to say no to me. I can almost see the two different sides of her head arguing with each other — the one who wants to encourage me to follow my dream versus the one who promised Dad and the doctors that she'd look after me and make sure I don't get worse.

"Look," I say, stuffing down more eggs and bacon. "Appetite back. See? And I feel a lot more energetic!"

That's a complete lie. My chest feels heavy and sore, and I'm exhausted.

Mom yawns and stands up. "Well, I don't," she says. "It's one o'clock. I suggest we both try to get some sleep. You said you wanted to go back to school in the morning. But I'm sorry — as far as New York goes, my decision is final."

My heart sinks toward the blue tiled floor.

"Sure, leave me with all the dishes," I mutter, but not loud enough for her to hear me. My mess — I'll need to clean it up. That's one of the many rules in this house.

I leave the dishes for now, and I haul myself up the stairs to reunite with my bed. "I hate you, CF," I say. "Why do you always have to ruin everything?"

I haven't even done my lung clearing yet.

I take a good snort of my special steroid inhaler to help with lung inflammation and to relieve tightness in my chest. Then I have to do my physical therapy. When I was little, Mom had to do the PT on me every single day, whacking me on the back and shoulders and tapping me on the sides in a special way so that all the gunk would come out of my lungs. Now that I'm older, I do my own PT by performing special controlled breathing exercises, but I still get a lot of chest infections, and I've missed a ton of school because I can't stop coughing and feeling out of breath.

I do forty minutes of tedious exercises, and then I lie in bed feeling sad for a while, and then the next thing I know it's morning and Harry has just texted to say he'll walk me to school if I'm going.

Harry.

Thank goodness for kind, sweet, handsome, romantic Harry.

He's kind of my salvation.

Totally Irresistible
Cheese Straws

To make 12, you will need:

- A little bit of butter or margarine
- ¾ cups plain flour
- A pinch of salt
- A pinch of cayenne pepper or mustard powder
- 3 tablespoons butter right from the fridge, chopped into little pieces
- 1 egg yolk
- ½ cup strong cheddar cheese, grated (the larger the flakes of grated cheese, the better)
- Some ice-cold water
- 1 tablespoon of grated Parmesan (optional)
- A pinch of dried sage or rosemary (optional)

First you need to heat up the oven to 400°F. Grease a baking tray with some butter or margarine.

Sieve the flour, cayenne or mustard powder, and salt into a bowl. If you like herbs, you could sprinkle in some dried sage or rosemary at this stage, too. Add the cubes of butter and work it all in with your fingertips, until you are left with a bowl of what looks like breadcrumbs.

With a spoon, mix in the egg yolk and the grated cheddar cheese and add a small amount of the cold water (you can chill it in the freezer in a bottle just before you need it). With your hands, knead the mixture into a smooth ball of dough. Put this in some plastic wrap and leave it in the fridge for about 10 to 15 minutes.

Put some flour on a cutting board or work surface and also on your rolling pin. Roll out your dough into a rectangle that's about an eighth of an inch thick. Then get a sharp knife and divide the rectangle into 12 long equal pieces.

Put them on the baking tray and into the hot oven for about 12 minutes, until they're golden and slightly puffy. You can sprinkle them with Parmesan if you like it (I don't) and then put them on a wire rack to cool down. Or you can eat them straight from the oven, like I do. And be warned — once you've eaten one, you will have to eat another! That's because they are so irresistible. *If* you manage to resist, you can store them in an airtight container or jar for a couple of days.

CHAPTER 6

"Ow," I say. I rub at the sore area on my chest where you can just make out the outline of my port beneath the skin. The port was put in over a year ago. It lives under the skin on my chest, and it makes it easier for the nurses to pump treatments through a tube and quickly into my body.

I'm at the special CF center. It's kind of like a hospital, but it's only for people with CF. There's a whole team of people here to help people like me. I've been coming here forever — ever since I was diagnosed when I was a tiny baby — and know everybody in the building. There's Dr. Rogers, the physician who's in charge of my health. Then there's Trish, the nurse. She does things like pump antibiotics into my port when I have a chest infection, and she takes special swab samples from me every few weeks to make sure I'm not getting a new infection. People with CF get tons of colds and coughs, same as everybody else, but if I get one, it can turn into something nastier and make my lungs even worse than they already are. So if I get even the slightest trace of a sniffle, Mom zooms me to the CF center and gets Trish to take a sample. If the results show that I have an infection, I'm pumped full of extra-strong antibiotics, sometimes for months. Trish also comes to our house if I'm feeling really sick. Mom and Trish are basically friends now — she's been part of our lives for so long.

I also see a lot of Diane. She's the dietician who advises me what to eat and when. There's Fiona, the social worker who helps Mom with school issues and tells her how to claim the special tax breaks and things she's entitled to for looking after me. And then there's Tom, the physical therapist. He taught Mom how to treat me at home with her hands to help loosen all the stubborn mucus in my chest. Two years ago, he taught me how to do something called autogenic drainage, which I can do on my own at home so that Mom doesn't need to get so involved with my PT anymore. For this I have to lie on my back on my bed and do three special kinds of breathing: unsticking, collecting, and evacuating the mucus out of my battered lungs. The noises I make while I am doing it are not pretty. I'm supposed to do it twice a day, but I always get in trouble with Mom because I tend to, uh, forget. Or life gets in the way. Or I don't really want Jenna stopping by in the middle of it, even though she's really good about the whole CF thing.

Or worst of all, I might have a batch of muffins to take out of the oven.

Flour Power!

***

So I'm at the CF center having my port flushed. I need to have this done every month to make sure that it doesn't get clogged, or else my antibiotics can't get into my system. It feels a little uncomfortable, but the main issue is that I just get so bored waiting for it all to be finished.

I'm in a room of my own. People with CF have to be very careful not to infect one another. That sucks. It's bad enough being in the hospital so often without being able to speak to people your own age who might just understand what you're going through.

I have a pile of food magazines on my lap, and I'm leafing through the latest recipes by Cat Cora, Alton Brown, and Mario Batali, while trying not to notice what's going on in my chest.

"She's been more sick this month than she has been in years," Mom is saying to Dr. Rogers, who has just walked into the room. I've known Dr. Rogers since I was about six.

"Hi, Dr. R," I say to him, flipping through the bright, glossy pages of *Food Network Magazine.* "How's it hanging?"

Mom sighs.

"Not a great question to ask a doctor," says Dr. Rogers. "I'm likely to give you a long, medical, and potentially boring answer."

I smile. I like Dr. Rogers and his weird sense of humor. Somehow he always manages to make me feel like Amelie-the-Person rather than just Amelie-the-Patient.

"Your mom tells me you want to go to New York City," he says. "Some big competition, I hear. That sounds very exciting."

"Yeah," I say, "but has she also told you that she's not letting me go?"

Mom flushes pink when I say that. Her face clashes with her red jacket. I think of the pink section in a carton of Neapolitan ice cream and the red of the strawberry sauce I like to pour over it.

"I was just about to get around to that," she says, all defensive and huffy. "Dr. Rogers is a very busy man."

He perches on the edge of the bed where I'm lying. "Not too busy to discuss your health," he says. "So I take it you still want to go to New York?"

I put down the magazines with a sigh. I just found a glorious twist on the traditional baked cheesecake recipe that involves a bunch of chocolate.

"Of course I do," I say. "It's only like the biggest baking competition in the country. And I don't see why I can't go still, as long as I'm careful and look after myself."

Mom stands up and folds her arms. She looks tired, wary, and wired all at the same time. "I'm getting a little fed up with this stuck record act," she says in a voice I hardly ever hear. "I've told you you're not going, and that's that. Don't try to make me change my mind by dragging Dr. Rogers into it."

Dr. Rogers stands up and clears his throat. "It's your annual checkup next week, isn't it?" he says. "If you're okay with it, Mrs. Day, maybe we could make a final decision based on the results of that?"

Mom flushes again. I can tell that she's angry that Dr. Rogers didn't back her up entirely. "Oh, all right," she says. "But I can't see Amelie being much better than she is now, and currently, she is in no state to be going anywhere. I'll be at the coffee machine." She leaves the room and lets the door bang shut behind her.

Dr. Rogers and I look at one another for a moment. He has kind eyes — dark like chocolate-covered raisins and with a sort of glint behind them. I try to picture what his kids are like and bet that he's a good father.

"I just want to get on with my life," I say in a whisper. "That's all."

Dr. Rogers nods and puts his hand on my shoulder for a moment. The brief gesture causes tears to well up in my eyes.

"I'll leave you in the capable hands of Nurse Anna," he says. The nurse is unhooking the tube from my port. "Don't worry. I'm sure we can figure something out."

My heart lifts a little.

"Oh, here," I call after his retreating back. "I made you something."

Dr. Rogers comes back and peels back the lid of the box I'm holding out.

"They're medical themed," I say shyly.

He bursts out laughing. I've been practicing cookies for the competition. Inside are some iced sugar cookies with

52

little piped pictures on top. I did a pair of lungs on one, a heart on another, and a selection of pills, beds, syringes, and stethoscopes on the rest. It took me half the night to perfect the drawings, and I did them in a dark green color, the same shade as Dr. Rogers's scrubs.

"You are something else, Amelie," he says, wiping his eyes. "I shouldn't eat these. They're too perfect. But of course, I will."

Then he leaves the room, still laughing to himself. I let the nurse clean me up and prepare me to go home.

***

Dad stops by to see me after I get home from the CF center.

I'm in the kitchen making mini carrot cakes with buttercream frosting. I've cut some carrot shapes out of my leftover fondant and colored them orange, and I'm just sticking these on top of the finished cakes.

In addition to these, I have already made a few batches of maple syrup cookies — my favorite kind. There's a pile of homework upstairs with my name on it, but after a day spent in the hot, disinfectant-smelling air of the hospital, I felt like letting my creative vision run wild, so I've ditched the idea of doing math until later.

"There," I say, standing back to admire my handiwork. The little square cakes stand at attention in neat lines on the rack, each one covered in fluffy buttercream frosting that

I've run a fork through to make peaks that look a little like snowdrifts.

"Yum!" says Dad, heading toward the rack with a purposeful look in his eye. "I think you need a second opinion on those from your Chief Taster."

I sigh. "Harry is Chief Taster," I say. "You can be Backup Taster, if you want."

Dad frowns. "I've been relegated to the sidelines," he says. "Wow. I hope I'm at least still your favorite dad."

I let him pick out a cake and watch him bite into the rich, spongy goodness.

"Good?" I ask. "I added some lemon juice just to make it a little different."

"Mm," says Dad with his cheeks bulging. "Excellent. And with carrots! I would love to see what you can do with a zucchini."

I smile and put the teakettle on the stove.

Mom comes downstairs and gives Dad a peck on the cheek. "Thought I heard you," she says. "Why don't you come outside and admire my petunias?"

"Oh, boy," says Dad. "How much more excitement can one man take?"

He winks at me and then heads outside with Mom. They walk around our back courtyard garden, staring into pots and planters and chatting avidly the whole time.

I make the tea and bang on the window, and they wave but don't come in.

I'm about to bang again, and then I realize what they're

doing — why Dad came over. They're discussing the New York question. They're talking about me.

For a moment, I feel a surge of anger. Then I swallow it down again. I know it's only because they care. But if they're talking about my future, then I really should be out there taking part in the discussion.

I put the three mugs on a tray and add three of my mini carrot cakes, and I head out back. Mom and Dad have stopped looking at plants. Mom is now facing Dad with her hands on her hips, which can't be a good thing — that's the position she adopts when she's yelling at me about something. Dad is staring at his feet and shuffling around, which is also not good.

I sigh and offer them the tray. "I know you're talking about me," I say, "which is why I came out here. Plus, I can't lip-read from that far away, which is kind of annoying."

Dad smiles when I say this. Mom doesn't.

"Sometimes your father and I need to talk about stuff in private," she says. "Couldn't you have given us another minute?"

I look at Dad. He shrugs and reaches for a mug of tea. "Your mom's in charge here," he says. "What she says goes."

He says this in a mechanical way, like he's rehearsed it. I look at him more closely. He doesn't look very pleased. I'm not sure whether he's annoyed with me for coming outside and interrupting or with Mom.

"Dad," I say. "What do *you* think about me going to New York? Honestly?"

Dad glances at Mom. She gives him an imploring sort of look, like she's trying to affect what he's about to say, but Dad sits down on the edge of a large pot full of orange marigolds and takes a gulp of his tea.

"Honestly?" he says. "I think it's a terrific idea."

"John!" says my mother in a shocked tone. "I thought we just agreed . . ."

Dad rubs his eyes and blinks. "I didn't agree to anything," he says. "You told me not to say something, but Mel asked me a direct question, and I'm going to give her a direct answer."

I look at my dad with new eyes full of respect, love, and a little fear. Doesn't he know that disagreeing with Mom can be like throwing a lit match into a room full of gas? Oh, yeah — he does. That's why they got divorced.

"Oh, for crying out loud," says Mom. "Thanks a bunch. You've just made the next few weeks a heck of a lot harder for me."

She looks really upset, like she's going to cry.

I get up and offer her the cake plate.

"Cake is not the answer to everything," she snaps. Then she looks at the tiny orange carrots with their green stems and relents. "Oh, fine — just one."

She eats it with an angry look on her face.

"For what it's worth," says Dad. "I happen to think that Mel doing this competition is a fantastic idea. Our beautiful, talented, and creative daughter has been offered an exciting opportunity that she'd be a fool to pass up. This is what her life should be like. Shouldn't we be supporting it? Do you remember what the counselor at the CF center said?"

I remember full well what the counselor said, because I'd been there too, and because it was the first thing that anybody at the center had ever said to me that made perfect, total sense.

The counselor said now that I was in my teens, Mom should stop acting so much like the "CF Police." She meant that Mom was trying too hard to control what I did because she was so anxious about my health. The counselor thought that keeping me from doing things I really wanted to do was having a far worse effect on me than just skipping a treatment or forgetting to take a pill.

Mom gets a folding chair out of the shed and sits down with a sigh. "Of course I remember," she says. "I'm proud that Amelie made it to the quarterfinals. I'm as excited by that as you are, John. But the fact remains that a week in New York City is going to be detrimental to her overall health. And isn't *that* our main concern? Dang, this carrot cake is good!"

I allow myself a small, victorious smile at that.

Mom locks eyes with Dad, and they have a kind of stare-off, like the black cat and the Siamese who are always passing through our yard in a flurry of teeth, eyes, yowls, and spits.

In the end, Dad gets up and puts his mug and plate back on the tray. "I don't think we're going to agree, are we?" he says. "You're more concerned with her physical health, and

I'm concerned with her mental health. How do we meet in the middle?"

Mom shakes her head. "We don't," she says in a tired voice. "I'm the one who lives with her. So I will make the decision. Okay?"

Dad nods, but his face looks sad. It mirrors my own. I can see my fabulous baking opportunity slipping even further into the great mixing bowl of life, to be lost in a mess of eggs, flour, and butter.

He gets up and walks back over to the cobblestones and out the gate toward his car. "See you, kiddo," he says, blowing me a kiss.

He blows one to Mom too, but she pretends not to see.

Wow. Parents can be so stressful. I feel so worn out from witnessing their conversation that I have to have another fortifying carrot cake and cup of tea.

"I guess that's it then," I say to Mom as we tidy up in the kitchen. "I should forget about going to New York."

My voice must sound sad, because Mom comes over and gives me a hug.

"I don't think you can go, honey," she says. "But if you want, we'll get your annual checkup over with and make a final decision. Okay?"

That's definitely progress. I give her a hug back and offer to cook dinner, which for me is like the biggest treat out there.

"Can I invite Harry over for dinner?" I say.

Mom smiles. "Okay," she says.

I watch her disappear upstairs, and I realize that she still has no intention of letting me go to New York. The annual checkup hardly ever brings good news. My lung function is always worse than the year before. I can feel it. I get more out of breath than I used to, and my coughing has taken on a new and deadly rattle. I'm dreading the part where the doctors measure my BMI, too. That stands for body mass index, and it determines whether I'm the right weight for my height. I've never once been the right weight, and the nutritionist always tells me that I need to pack more calories into my diet.

I sink down onto the stairs and bury my face in my arms.

I have to go to New York.

I just have to.

The rest of my life depends on it.

Maple Syrup Cookies

To make about 30 of these delicious, chewy cookies, you will need:

- 2 cups all-purpose flour
- 1 stick butter
- 1 cup packed brown sugar
- ¾ cup maple syrup
- 1 egg
- 1 teaspoon vanilla extract
- ½ teaspoon baking soda
- ½ teaspoon salt
- ½ teaspoon cinnamon
- ½ teaspoon ground ginger
- ½ cup sliced almonds (optional)

First of all, you need to leave the butter out until it is at room temperature. Then combine it with the brown sugar in a mixing bowl. Cream the butter and brown sugar together until it is light and fluffy. Add the egg, syrup, and vanilla and beat well.

In a separate mixing bowl, sieve your flour, add the baking soda, ginger, cinnamon, and salt, and mix this together. Then pour in the wet ingredient mixture and stir until you have a firm cookie dough. I like them best plain, but if you want, you can add sliced almonds.

Place the dough in the refrigerator to cool for one hour.

When the cookie dough has chilled for an hour, preheat the oven to 350°F.

Shape the mixture into balls just bigger than a golf ball and place them on a couple of greased cookie sheets. You will need to leave a fair amount of space around each cookie because when they cook, they spread out a bunch and could end up combined with the next cookie! It's probably best to limit the number to 10 cookies per sheet. If you have any dough left over, refrigerate it and roll it out to make more cookies in a day or two.

Bake them in the oven for about 10–12 minutes or until they are firm to the touch. When they come out, let them cool on a wire rack and then store in an airtight container.

CHAPTER 7

I miss five days of school.

Trish's latest sample shows that I have another chest infection brewing, and I need to take more antibiotics in addition to the ones I take every day by inhaling from my nebulizer. Trish showed Mom how to put the new stronger drugs into a tube that feeds in through my port, so she does this every day while I lie on the couch and complain about not being able to make cakes. I read recipe books instead, one after another, and start scribbling down pages of ideas.

I glance at the list of rules from the competition organizers. For the two desserts, I have to make some mini-dessert and then a larger one. I'm agonizing between mini dark chocolate lava cakes with Chantilly crème or rich, moist mini apple tarts with homemade almond ice cream. For the larger cake, I'm pretty sure I'm going to do my famous German gingerbread with vanilla custard.

So I wait until the fourth day, when I've started to feel a

little better, and I go back into the kitchen and start messing around with flour and sugar and eggs. Mom comes home from work and does a big, blissful sniff of the air and tries not to look at the smeared work surfaces, the flour all over the floor, and the knives covered in butter and flung into bowls.

"I hope you're not overdoing it," Mom says.

I make a face. We've only recently started speaking again, Mom and I. We have a pretty intense relationship at the best of times. She's the only one who sees me when I'm really sick, and she's the one who has to deal with it. Sometimes I don't even want to look at her worried, tired face anymore, because it just reminds me of how sick I am.

The day before yesterday, she tried to put her arm around me while she held a bowl in front of my face for me to cough stuff into, and I pushed her away. Hard. The bowl fell to the floor and Mom jumped like she'd been shot, but then she saw my face and chest contorting with the effort of getting all the mucus up, and her face softened. She sat next to me on the edge of the bed, taking care not to touch me that time, and she held the bowl until I'd finished. Then she carried it to the bathroom and cleaned it out, got me a glass of water, and made me a bowl of thick mushroom soup with a swirl of cream on top for dinner.

"You need to eat it," she'd said. "You're getting too thin again."

I still felt sick, but I sipped the soup and a faint color crept back into my white face.

Mom is amazing. And I know she is, which makes me feel really horrible when I'm mean to her and yell at her.

Sometimes I tell her to get the heck out of my bedroom.

***

It's two days until my annual checkup.

I'm back at school for a half-day because I'm tiring really easily now, and Mom wants me home right after lunch. It's kind of tough dipping in and out of school like this. I feel like I miss out on a lot of stuff — even the gossip. My classmates don't give me a hard time about it, and some of them make a point of asking me how I am, but I still feel like I stick out like a sore lung.

It doesn't help that I'm smaller and thinner than most of the kids in my grade. Despite that, I'm a pretty key member of the school's soccer team. Because I'm small and wiry, I can dodge the other players and hold on to the ball.

I play a little at morning soccer practice after using my inhaler, and then I sit through two classes. By the time the bell rings for lunch, I feel pretty wiped out. I don't tell anybody. There are teachers who look out for me, and if I told them I was feeling bad, they'd send me to the school nurse and she'd call Mom right away.

"You okay?" Harry asks. We're walking toward the back of the school to eat our lunch underneath the big oak tree near the playing fields, and the short walk feels like miles to me. Since Harry's in the grade above me, we don't see each other at school much. We only eat lunch together twice a week for half an hour because he has tennis during lunch break on Tuesdays and judo on Thursdays, and I have art club on Friday at lunchtime, so it's kind of special being able to sit underneath the tree with him.

"Yeah. Ish," I say, sitting down on the damp grass and leaning back against the tree trunk with a sigh. I'm more honest with Harry than I am with anybody else on the planet, even Jenna. There's something about Harry that makes me more patient with him than I am with anyone else in my life. I think it's because he's pretty casual and normal about the whole CF thing. That doesn't mean he doesn't care. He keeps a sharp eye on me, but he's the opposite of the "CF Police." He lets me express opinions and do things I want to do without warning me constantly that whatever it is will make my CF worse.

I open my lunchbox. Then a fit of coughing takes hold of me, and I lean forward and cough and retch and make revolting rattling noises from my chest until I'm aching with tiredness.

"Sorry," I whisper. "I hate this cough sometimes."

Harry nods. Then he snaps open his lunchbox and reveals a ton of healthy stuff, like apples and a salad. He knows full well that he's going to get half of my cake and chocolate supply, so his lunch is not as healthy as it looks.

"Trade?" he says, holding out a tub of cucumber and tomato and eyeing the lemon muffins that I made last night. They're drizzled with icing made with fresh lemons, and

65

there's a sharp lemon syrup running through the sponge of each little cake so that biting into them is all zingy and surprising and tickles the insides of your cheeks.

"Ha, ha," I say. I take one piece of cucumber and pass the rest of the salad back to him. I can't eat tomatoes because my stomach already makes too much acid, and they just make it worse. Then I give him one of the muffins and keep two for myself. I'm not being greedy — I just need to cram in the calories or else I'll get even thinner.

"So," says Harry, not looking me in the eye but frowning over at the science lab like he's waiting for something to explode out of the roof, "are you feeling really bad today?"

I sigh and put the Tupperware down on my lap. I finish chewing and make a mental note to add slightly less sugar to the lemon syrup next time, and then I rest my head on his warm shoulder.

"Oh, I don't know," I say, sniffing the starchy smell of his polo shirt. Harry's mother is really into fragrant fabric softener with pictures of tulips on the bottle. "Kind of. Better than I felt three days ago. But I'm dreading my checkup."

Harry rests his cheek on the top of my head for a moment and then bites into his apple. He takes such a huge bite that half the apple disappears into his mouth right away.

"Have you had your thingy?" he says. He's looking at my backpack.

I make a face. "You sound like Mom," I say. "Except she would refer to it by its correct name."

Harry laughs. "Okay, then — have you had your Creon?"

he says, passing me the backpack. "Leave it to you to take something that sounds like a character from *Star Trek*."

I get out my plastic box of pills and take a few of the enzymes that I need to take with every meal. I gulp down some water and then lean back and look up at the clouds drifting in the sky.

"Harry," I say. My voice sounds clogged. I reach into the bag, pull out my inhaler, and take a few deep breaths on it. Better. "Where do you think we go when we die?"

Harry gives me a startled look when I say that. He tries to cover it up right away by leaning forward and fiddling with the laces on his shoes, but I saw his face lose the smiley look for a moment, and a tiny, mean part of me feels pleased that I actually mean that much to him.

"Dunno," he says. "Not sure we really go anywhere. Why? Do you want to go somewhere else?"

I shiver and pull the sleeves of my cardigan down. It's cooling down out here, and lots of kids are heading back inside because the bell is going to ring any minute. I'm one of the few kids who doesn't rush anywhere at school, and I'm often slightly late for class. It's not because I'm trying to be a rebel or anything cool like that. It's because if I rush, I get out of breath and enter the classroom in a fit of coughing. Let's face it, I might as well have a flashing red light on my head and a sign saying, *SICK PERSON* in big letters around my neck if my cough starts up in the classroom. Once I'm coughing, class always comes to a halt. I don't think that the teachers can hear themselves talk over the racket.

You might think that a person with CF would want to rush more, because they know that their life is likely to be a whole lot shorter than everybody else's, but I'm not really like that, even though sometimes I want to try to pack as many experiences into my life as possible.

I watch the rest of my class rush inside, as I take a deep breath and stand up. It's like I already know what life's about, and this urgent rush to get everywhere seems kind of stupid. I mean, I know that life is short and goes fast, even for people who live to be eighty. So sometimes I like to lean back and take a look at things and really notice them. After all, I don't have too much time left to notice things, do I?

"I've just been thinking about it a lot," I say, walking slowly beside Harry. "Sorry. I didn't mean to be all gruesome and morbid. Kind of stupid, huh?"

I turn to look at Harry with a grin on my face, but for once he doesn't return it. Instead he kicks at the wall outside the main school entrance. When he turns to me, his face is red and ugly.

"Mel," he says, "you're thirteen. Yeah, I know you have a life-threatening illness. I know that, and I accept it. But all this stuff about life after death is getting to me, all right? Maybe I don't want to think about you not being around. Have you ever tried to look at this from *my* point of view?"

He flings open the double doors so hard that they bang against the walls and slam back, nearly injuring a couple of girls from my grade.

"Sorry," I say to the girls. They scowl at me and raise

their eyebrows at one another. I wouldn't blame them if they were thinking, *There goes the pathetic sick girl who can't get anything right.*

Tears threaten to spill out of my eyes, so I fumble in my pocket for a Snickers bar and shove it savagely into my mouth.

I go into the girl's bathroom and sit in a stall. I cough until my eyes are watering yet again.

Then I close my eyes and put my head in my hands and wish I were somebody else.

CHAPTER 8

Sometimes I dream up recipes in the night.

I keep a pen and notebook by my bed just in case I get any brilliant ideas. The cakes I invent in my sleep are often a lot more colorful and unusual than the ones I cook up when I'm awake.

Jenna's always telling me that she dreams about guys on *The Bachelorette*, or else she dreams that she hasn't finished her math homework and her teacher is yelling at her.

Those dreams sound a little boring to me.

I dream about lavender icing and white chocolate chips. I dream of caramel sauce being poured from an enormous jug onto a giant molasses cake. I dream of huge vats of whipped cream and enormous bags of rainbow sprinkles pouring out over my head and raining down on my body. I once dreamed that I was being chased through a field by a giant brown cupcake with stick legs and big waving hands, but I'm not sure what that meant.

Anyway, it's a safe bet that most nights when I close my eyes, some sort of cake is going to show up in my dreams.

I never, ever dream about my illness. I guess I live so much of it during the day that my subconscious doesn't really need to explore it during the night. That's why I like being asleep so much. When I'm asleep, it's like the CF doesn't exist.

The night before my annual checkup it takes me hours to fall asleep.

When I finally drift off, exhausted, in the early hours, I don't dream at all.

But that scares me more than any nightmare I might have had.

It's like being dead.

***

Mom insists we have a good breakfast even though my insides are really sore and my stomach is churning and making weird noises.

"It'll be a very long day for you today, Amelie," she says. "You need some energy."

I give a feeble snort. I can barely sit up straight at the table after my bad night. I can't help thinking back to my last annual checkup when I went for a run around the block before we headed off to the CF center and spent the whole day bouncing off the clinic walls with frustration, desperate to get home and bake.

Today I almost feel like it would be a relief to spend some time lying around in the CF center doing nothing. I haven't spoken to Harry since he got angry two days ago, and he hasn't texted me, which is really out of character. Jenna says that boys need to go off and have sulking time on their own and that he'll come out of his cave when he's ready. But I'm not so sure.

I hate not speaking to Harry. It's like the rug has been pulled out from under my feet. He's my support system. He even offered to come with me to all my medical appointments once, but I've never let him. It's bad enough that Mom has to see me at my worst without Harry having to see that, too. Something about tall, fresh-faced, glowing, athletic Harry would look wrong against the clinical whiteness of the sterile hospital rooms where I spend so much of my time.

"Take it off the heat," I say to Mom. She's attempting to make scrambled eggs, but she's never quite gotten the technique right. She always leaves them on the stove for so long that they get dry and rubbery and split into hundreds of little pieces. I like my scrambled eggs soft, yellow, and creamy, and to get that result, you have to take the pan away from the heat before they've finished cooking.

"I don't want you to get salmonella," says Mom, but she starts spooning the egg onto some of my homemade whole wheat bread. She puts two plates in front of us and pours me a mug of tea.

"Ugh, this is weak tea," I say in an automatic way, staring at the orangey scum floating at the top of my mug.

Mom ignores me. She's used to me making a fuss about the way everything is done in the kitchen.

She has the day off work today and is dressed in leggings and a floaty top instead of her usual smart business suit and heels. Even though she's kind of old, she somehow manages to look trendy. If some of the other mothers of kids at school wore leggings, they'd look kind of sad.

I can tell that she's really worried. I can hear it in her overly bright voice and see it in the way she keeps staring up at the clock.

She's been to every single one of my annual checkups and has seen how things have started to slide downward a little more every year. Dad comes to them, too, whenever he can take time away from work. If he can't make it, Mom calls him at the end of the day, and they discuss my results over the phone.

I sigh as I force the scrambled egg down into my sore guts.

"Creon," says Mom. She pushes my pillbox across the table. I take a few of the capsules and gulp them down with the weak tea.

"Aspirin," she says next. I glance up, surprised.

"I don't take aspirin," I say. "Do I?"

I take so many pills, sometimes I'm not sure what they all are.

Mom smiles. "The aspirin is for me," she says. "I always get a headache at the CF center. It's the stress of waiting around in those stuffy rooms."

She slips a small white bottle into her handbag and stands up. "Okay," she says. "Let's go and get this over with, and then we can come back home."

***

We're at the CF center by 8:30. I have several different staff to see over the course of the day and numerous tests. They estimate I'll be at the hospital until the early evening, so Mom has packed up a huge bag full of high-calorie drinks and snacks to keep me going. Plus she has my inhaler, my nebulizer, and a box of bandages in case the skin around my port snags and bleeds.

The first thing I'm having done is a series of blood tests to make sure I'm not getting liver disease or anything else that could affect my organs. We sit in a gray waiting room with a bunch of bored-looking people and wait for almost a half hour to get called in. I roll up my sleeve and let the nurse extract my dark blood into a series of little tubes. It comes out cherry-red and glossy, which gets me thinking about red cherry icing on cupcakes, and I get so excited about this new icing I haven't tried that I don't even hear what the nurse is saying to me until Mom nudges me. I press the gauze to the hole in my arm, and the nurse places a bandage over it.

The easy part is done.

The next thing I need to have done is a CT scan. This is so that the doctors can see my lungs and whether my airways have been damaged by repeated chest infections. I usually only get this once a year at my checkup.

I have to lie inside a tunnel for the scan. When I first had this done, I got really panicky being in the dark, enclosed space, but I've had so many of them now that I don't even think about it. When it's over, the radiographer lets me take a look on her computer screen. Not everybody gets to see their images right away, but I know all the staff in this place, so I'm allowed to.

"Hmm," I say, staring at my ribs on the picture. My port is visible, too — a tiny circle at the top of my chest. "I look like a rack of lamb."

Mom laughs. "She translates everything into food terms," she says to the radiographer. "It's her way of coping."

I give Mom an angry look. "No, it's not," I mumble. "I just think I look like ribs, that's all."

In fact, I'm trying not to look at the strange inflated shape of my chest on the scan. I know full well that this is not good. As if she's sensing my despair, the radiographer switches off her machine, and my ribs disappear from view.

A man in green scrubs comes in and puts me in a wheelchair to take me upstairs to the physical therapy department.

"I can walk, you know!" I protest, but deep down I'm relieved to be pushed. The CF center has tons of long, shiny gray corridors and the radiology department is miles from all the other offices. I'm out of breath already today. I'm not sure whether it's because I'm nervous or because I didn't sleep, but my energy levels feel like they might be hitting an all-time low.

Great.

Tom comes to greet me in the physical therapy department with his usual wide, white smile.

"Hi, Mel," he says. "How's it going?"

I don't think he really expects an answer to this, because he's already turned his back to me and is leading us to his office, but I give a weak smile and allow the hospital orderly to help me out of my chair.

Tom makes me lie on the couch and show him how I'm doing my autogenic drainage. I demonstrate my amazing breathing techniques, and Mom tries not to wince at the ghastly rattling of the mucus clearing from my airways.

"Okay," he says afterward. "Are you still doing it twice a day?"

I nod. Mom gives me a harsh look until I'm forced to look down at my feet.

"I might forget sometimes," I mutter. "Lots of homework, you know."

Tom smiles, but the smile looks like one of concern.

"I think you need to really make sure you do it, Mel," he says. "And I haven't seen your CT scan results yet, but by the sounds of it, we need to increase the number of times you do the breathing to at least three times a day."

I groan and bury my head on the desk for a moment.

When I come up, I get dizzy for a moment and clutch at the sides of my chair.

I can see Mom trying not to panic.

"I'm fine," I say. I sit up straight and force a smile. "Okay. I'll do it three times a day. Promise."

Mom and Tom exchange a few more ideas and concerns while I sit there bored, staring at the pamphlet stand in his office and trying to make cake words out of "cystic fibrosis." I'm still struggling with that when Mom drags me off for my next two appointments.

I'm kind of dreading these two.

The first is with the nutritionist, Diane. She's the cleanest woman in the world. Her white coat is spotless and her shiny brown hair is tied back into a neat knot. Her glasses sparkle, and her shoes are polished nicely. Her office is very bare and tidy, with two identical potted plants placed at each end of the windowsill. I bet if Diane passed through our kitchen after I made a cheesecake, she would have a heart attack from just looking at the mess.

"Okay," she says, sitting behind her desk and gesturing for Mom and me to sit down. "I can see that you've lost a little weight, Amelie, since you last came in."

I last came in about four months ago, so this is not such good news.

Diane weighs me on her digital scales and then measures my height. She calculates my body mass index, dividing my weight by my height.

"You're quite a lot less than you should be," she says. "Have you been getting your maximum calories in every day?"

I nod. This, at least, is true. Mom can't fault me on that one. I've been stuffing my face with cake, chocolate, and cookies on top of normal meals for what feels like forever.

"Hmm," says Diane. "I'm going to suggest something to help with your weight, but I don't want you to panic, okay?"

Why is it that as soon as somebody medical says the words "don't panic," you immediately want to scream and panic and thrash around?

I feel cold and thin. The weight of whatever she's about to suggest is already hovering over my head, about to plunge down and change my life yet again. I glance at Mom. She's gripping her hands together so hard that they have turned white, and she's fiddling with the finger where her wedding ring used to be, except of course it's no longer there.

"It's all right," says Diane. "Lots of people with CF have this. I'm going to suggest that you get set up with a feeding tube at home to pump calories into you overnight while you sleep. It really won't affect you when you're awake at all."

I blow out my lips in despair, forgetting that I can't breathe very well as it is. The short dip in oxygen leaves me coughing my guts up for almost five minutes. Diane gets a cardboard bowl and holds it under my mouth while Mom hovers around, chewing her lip and looking agonized.

When I've finished, I sit up again, exhausted.

"Sorry," I say. "You were talking about the tube. How would it go into my body?"

"Through your stomach via a gastrostomy," says Diane. "You'd have to have that put in under general anesthesia.

Then it would just stay in your stomach, closed off by a button during the day. It would be easy for you or your mom to connect the tube at night. We could get about two thousand more calories into you while you're sleeping."

I nod. It's amazing the things I've had to get used to over the years. I guess one more tube isn't going to make much of a difference. I still feel scared about it, though. Not so much about the tube, but what it means about the general direction my health is taking.

Diane gets me to fill out some forms saying that I'd like to be admitted to out-patient surgery to have the gastrostomy fitted, and then Mom helps me walk to the next appointment because I'm feeling tired and wobbly.

"Oh, poor baby," she says, squeezing my arm as we walk along. "Bet you can't wait to get home. I think we'll get a movie tonight and maybe have some pizza. Okay?"

I know she's trying to be kind and cheer me up, but it's not really working. All I can think about is the competition in two weeks and the fact that I've hardly prepared for it, and all I can see up ahead of me is a huge black mountain blocking my way to New York. Of course, being me, the mountain is made out of thousands of black olives all gleaming and glistening with oil and dotted with chili powder and garlic, but even this dramatic image fails to cheer me up much.

We've reached the office next door to Dr. Rogers, my physician, now. Trish is already there. She's going to do my lung function test, and then Mom and I are going to have a late lunch and then wait a couple of hours while Dr. Rogers gets all my results together and gives me his opinion on them.

The lung function test is the thing I dread most of all. It's really simple. All I have to do is blow hard into a machine, and it measures the volume of air blown out of my lungs. Trish then compares this number to the number she recorded when I last did the test, and then she can tell if my lung function has gotten better or worse.

I breathe as hard as I can into her machine, and as usual, it leaves me coughing and breathless, so we go through the whole process of Trish holding a bowl under my mouth and Mom pacing back and forth across the room. Then Trish gestures for me to sit down.

I can see by her sympathetic face that it's not great news.

"Yep, you guessed it," she says. "Your lung function is down quite a bit since last year's checkup. It's only at forty-eight percent, as opposed to last time when you were at almost sixty. We'll get the CT scan results, and then Dr. Rogers will be able to talk to you about what we might be able to do next. Okay?"

Trish is really nice, so I give her a big smile, even though my heart is aching at the news and I can't even look at Mom.

"You should get some better candy for CF patients," I say, pointing to the sad pile of fruit lollipops that she keeps to give to the little kids. "There aren't enough calories in those. You should be handing out fudge made with condensed milk. I'll whip some up for you next time."

Trish laughs. "Good point," she says. "See you later."

Then Mom and I stagger off downstairs to find the cafeteria.

The cafeteria in the CF center serves hot meals and sandwiches and also sells tons of high-calorie junk food, so Mom piles up my tray with shepherd's pie, roasted potatoes, and green beans and adds a strawberry milk shake and a piece of pound cake.

She chooses a Caesar salad for herself.

"I think I'd rather have yours," I say, eyeing the small meal with envy. My guts feel like they're twisted in knots, and I've got a faint feeling of nausea, not helped by the strong smell of hospital disinfectant all over the place.

"Tough," says Mom. "You heard what Diane said. You're losing way too much weight. So you need to eat this."

Mom is going into "CF Police" mode again, but I'm too tired to argue. I pick up the fork and examine the mixture of meat and mashed potato that I'm about to put into my mouth.

"Packet gravy," I say dolefully. When I cook shepherd's pie, I make an amazing gravy with fresh sage, homemade lamb stock, and a dash of Mom's favorite red wine when she's not looking. "And cheap potatoes, not Red Bliss. Yuck."

Mom sighs. "Oh, Amelie," she says. "You're funny. Only you could be complaining about the gravy when you've just gotten all that difficult news to digest. Most kids don't care what potatoes they're eating as long as they're made into fries."

I prod at my over-salted meal and consider this. "Mother," I say, "you of all people should know by now that I am not Most Kids."

Mom gives me a look that is hard to read for a moment, and then I realize that she can't speak because if she did, she'd start to cry.

I give her a weak smile, and we eat the rest of our lunch in silence.

***

After another two hours of hanging around drinking endless cups of tea and coffee and high-calorie milk shakes, Dr. Rogers finally comes out of his office and calls us in.

"Sorry you had such a long wait," he says. "I had to wait for the various results to come in from other departments. We want to make sure that we've got all the information before we talk to you." He ushers us into his office. Since he's an attending physician, he's got fancier furniture and much larger potted plants than everybody else. I sink down into the soft leather armchair, and Mom takes the one next to me.

"Okay, hit me with it," I say, before Dr. Rogers can start trying to dress up what he's about to say with lots of medical speak. "I've got some cake pans at home waiting for action."

Dr. Rogers's kind eyes twinkle at me over the top of his glasses, then he turns his attention to the files on his desk.

"There's the usual evidence of mild liver disease," he says. "Nothing to worry about at this stage. And all the other blood tests came back fine. But your lung function is down since last time, and your loss of weight is significant. I hear Diane spoke to you about gastrostomy. Do you have any questions about that?"

I shake my head. I've got a pamphlet about it in my bag, and I kind of understand the idea behind it.

"What about my lungs?" I ask. "Do I need to do even more PT? Tom said three times a day would be enough."

Dr. Rogers exchanges a quick look with Mom. Then he clicks on a machine next to his desk and holds up my chest scan so that I can see it lit up again. He points to an area of crisscrossing lines in front of my ribs. "See these?" he asks. "Because you've had chronic infection in your airways, they're now full of infected mucus and there's air trapped in your lungs, which is why your chest looks expanded. The long word for this is 'bronchiectasis.' The worse it gets, the more trouble your lungs will have clearing carbon dioxide from your bloodstream."

"Wow," I say. "Another long word for my collection. Thanks, Doc."

Mom flinches at my casual way of addressing Dr. Rogers.

"How do we stop it from getting worse?" she asks. "Is it a question of more physical therapy?"

Dr. Rogers takes off his glasses and rubs his brow for a moment. He looks tired. I wonder how many patients with CF he sees a day and whether they're all wisecracking and sarcastic like me, or whether he has kids weeping and sobbing all over his desk. I note that he's got a box of white tissues with the top one sticking out in my direction like he has predicted I'm going to need it.

Tissues always remind me of the rice paper I stick underneath my world-famous almond macaroons. I love macaroons, the way when you bite into them they're chewy instead of crisp. I love the way that the sugar slightly grates the roof of your mouth while it dissolves and then there's the strange delight of eating edible paper from the bottom of the cookie.

"No, not really," he says. "Of course, you need to keep doing the therapy — that's very important. But further deterioration of your lungs is hard for us to prevent. You soon may find it hard to walk anywhere without oxygen, and I'm guessing that's going to have quite an impact on your quality of life, as well as on your schoolwork."

I picture the soccer team, and a lump forms in my throat. Then I picture myself traveling to New York on the train for the competition, only the girl I'm picturing is bursting with vibrant health and doesn't have CF at all. She's a little on the plump side, but toned and athletic too. Her hair is thick, glossy, and healthy rather than dry and limp from a lack of nutrients. She's a little taller than I am — well, a lot taller. She's almost as tall as a supermodel. Her skin is back to a normal light olive color instead of pasty white, and when she takes a deep breath, she smiles and relaxes instead of bursting into fits of rattling cough. The only things she has to worry about are baking her best and looking good on TV.

Oh, shoot. Now my eyes are tearing up. I can't even look at Mom. I know exactly what her face will look like. She'll be biting her lip to try to stay in control and sensible and adult. Her eyes will be kind of imploring Dr. Rogers to say something helpful and positive and not-too-scary.

We both know what he's going to say next. He said it last year at my annual checkup, too, only then he said that we probably had another year or two before we needed to seriously consider it.

"I think we should speak again about putting you on the transplant list," he says.

And with that, the entire bottom falls out of my world, except that the way I see it in my head is somebody getting a huge sack of flour and then stabbing it at the bottom with a big knife so that all the flour trickles out and blows away.

"Mel, what do you think?" says Mom, reaching out to hold my hand.

They wait for me to answer.

But I can't speak.

***

On the way home, I eat a Twix bar in the passenger seat while Mom negotiates the rush-hour traffic. The CF center is only ten miles from where we live. Mom had location in mind when she chose the house we live in now, but with the traffic it takes an hour to get back.

Neither of us says much in the car.

There's really not much to say.

After Dr. Rogers mentioned the transplant, we spent a good amount of time in his office talking it all through, and we decided that I would have to put my name on the list.

I don't have much choice really.

If I want to live for a while longer, I have to have it done. Time is running out.

Mom puts on her turn signal and pulls in through the old arch and into our parking space at the back.

We sit in the car in silence for a moment, trying to find the right words.

In the end, I try to make light of it because Mom looks so upset.

"I suppose New York's a no-go, then?" I say. My voice sounds like a baby lamb, all thin and bleating. The thought of lamb makes a thin rush of hunger rise up in my chest, despite everything. Maybe I'll see if there's any ground lamb in the freezer and make burgers instead of having pizza. Burgers with blue cheese melted on top and thick, chunky fries and homemade ketchup. Yum.

Mom turns to face me. She takes both my hands in her thin, cold ones. "Yes, Amelie," she says. "I'm really sorry, but you're just not up for it right now. New York is most definitely not happening. End of story."

She gets out of the car.

I follow her inside in silence.

CHAPTER 9

After the checkup, I spend a week feeling miserable.

My health continues to get worse. I struggle for breath, and it's an effort to get to school. The school nurse keeps an eye on me, but she doesn't have time to single out one pupil for special attention, so mostly I monitor my own health and take pills and puffs from my inhaler whenever I think I need them. I ride the bus home and walk slowly down the road from the bus stop feeling like an old lady, tired and out of breath. Sometimes Jenna walks with me. When I told her about the checkup, I could see the sympathy in her eyes mixed with relief that it wasn't all happening to her. I suppose most people who know me feel like that, so I can't really blame her.

I've been having some thoughts about Jenna, and I don't like where they are going. I've admitted to myself that I'm the tiniest bit jealous of her being so healthy all the time. She never even seems to catch a cold. But she's my best friend, so when I have these thoughts, I feel swamped with guilt and self-loathing.

They've scheduled the surgery to fit my gastrostomy so that I can have night feedings through a tube. It's for next week — the day I was due to go to New York.

I guess it doesn't really matter now. I have to have the tube, and that's that.

And as for the lung transplant, I just have to wait.

I could be waiting for years. A lot of people are on the waiting list, and I need both lungs replaced — not just one. I try not to think about what getting a new pair of lungs means, but it's hard not to.

It means that somebody else will have to die so I can breathe again.

That's one heck of a thought to carry around. I start to worry that if I have a different pair of lungs, I won't be me any longer. What if I take on the personality of the girl or boy who has died? What if they hated baking? What if I lose my Flour Power?

The thought is too terrifying to spend much time on.

And there's another thing that's making me sad.

I still haven't heard from Harry.

***

I hang around the house all weekend, annoying Mom by making a mess in the kitchen and coming up with dramatic statements about lung transplants, until she eventually goes out shopping with a friend and leaves me alone for a couple of hours with strict instructions to call her cell if I start to feel worse. The door shuts behind her and it feels good for a moment to finally have her out of my hair, but then the silence starts cutting in, and I wander around the house coughing and looking out the windows and wondering if I'll ever hear from Harry again.

There's nothing good on TV so I reach for my laptop and go on Facebook for a while, and then I don't know what makes me do this, because I know full well that the whole New York thing is off and that Mom is expecting me to write to the competition organizers and tell them, but I go to my blog and I see with a little thrill that there are twenty-six new replies to my post calling for recipes. I click on the first one. It's from somebody called Jules. This is what it says:

Just saw your blog post and wanted to wish you luck if you do get to the New York competition. I'm one of the other people who applied, but I didn't make it, so I wondered if you'd like one of my recipes? You said you were looking for a cookie recipe, right? Well, I'm letting you have my fantastic recipe for chewy macaroons. It's handed down from my grandmother. She's kind of crazy, but I know she would be so happy if you baked her recipe in the competition. Hope you win!

— Jules

Macaroons! They only happen to be my most favorite cookie in the entire world!

I scroll down the page and look at the recipe, my eyes glinting and my heart pounding. I print it off and then read the rest of the replies on my blog. Most of them are from teenage girls, but one or two are from boys. That's really cool, that some boys have gone to the trouble of getting recipes from their families for me. There are a ton of recipes for sticky, gooey cakes, including gingerbread and double chocolate brownies — yum. And somebody has even taken up my challenge to make a chocolate lava cake and has posted a fuzzy photograph of chocolate sauce oozing out of soft, spongy cake.

Lots of people have expressed their disappointment that I might not be able to go to the competition. Yeah. Tell me about it. So I post a reply to every person who posted a recipe for me. I print out all the recipes and am about to go downstairs and lie on the couch with them and a big red pen, when a new response right at the top of the page catches my eye.

Dear Mel,

You sound nice, so I thought I'd give you one of my recipes. This is how you make it. You take one amazing, special girl who happens to have CF and you introduce her to a stupid idiot boy who forgets about all the good times that he has had with the amazing girl. Throw in his complete obsession with her awesome cupcakes and mix together. The end result should be that the girl and the boy live in perfect harmony, but the boy got the recipe wrong and burned it. Or it curdled. Or whatever cake mix does — I mean, how would I know? Anyway, hope you can use the recipe. Oh, and SORRY.

— H xoxo

My eyes well up with tears.

Then I pick up my phone, find him on speed dial, and wait for his lovely, kind voice to answer.

***

Something happens to me that evening.

After I speak to Harry and he says he's missed me and he's sorry (again), I feel all fired up and strange and a little bit reckless.

Mom comes back home laden with shopping bags, and we get out all the clothes she bought and try them on. She got me some new black leggings and a pretty, summery tunic in white with red roses on it.

"It's perfect, Mom," I say, twirling in front of the mirror and then stopping to cough. "Thanks. And I'm sorry I've been a nightmare daughter this week."

"Only this week?" says Mom, but her eyes are shining in a mischievous sort of way.

She brought home a box of old-fashioned doughnuts, too, and we devour them at the kitchen table, each of us with a cup of rich, spicy chai. For once we don't talk about how my own recipes would be better or about CF or the competition or school, but just enjoy cramming the fried goodness into our mouths and licking the sticky glaze off our lips.

"It's nice having a daughter who doesn't nag me about extra calories," says Mom, reaching for another doughnut and undoing her brown leather belt. "I might even order some Chinese later, too. What do you think?"

"Great," I say, but I'm not really listening.

I don't know whether it's the doughnuts, or the kindness of all the strangers with their recipes, or the fact that I've been resting at home for days, or that Harry was so sweet on the phone and I'm relieved that we're going out again, or maybe even that deep down I realize I might soon be getting a lung transplant and am going to be out of action for ages — but my brain is doing all these strange, devious little things that I can't voice to Mom. The more I try to ignore them, the bigger and more powerful they seem to get, until I feel like I'm going to burst if I don't go upstairs to my bedroom and give them some serious thought.

"I'm tired," I lie as we clear the table. "I think I'll go rest in bed for a while. I'll get up for dinner, though. Don't worry."

"Oh," says Mom. Her jolly voice has faded to the concerned one again. "Are you sure you're okay? You never go to sleep this early."

"Yeah," I say. "I'm just going to lie down and watch TV in my room, that's all."

"Oh, right," says Mom. Her smile returns. "One of your horrible reality TV shows, I bet."

"Of course," I say. "Or a cooking show. That's new, right?"

Mom laughs and takes her bags upstairs. I follow her and go into my room.

I shut the door and wait until she's downstairs again, and I hear her chatting on the phone with my grandmother.

Then I open my laptop and start to plan.

CHAPTER 10

For the next five days I go about my usual business, but I've got this bubbling excitement inside me, and it's all I can do not to blurt it out to somebody.

It's like the secret I'm carrying around has given me a new burst of energy. I go to school full-time all week, and I play in another soccer game and only need my inhaler once after the game and not before like I usually do. I go see a movie with Harry after school on Wednesday, and I sit snuggled up under his arm in the back row, and I feel like I might die of happiness and excitement rather than from CF, which is a new way of looking at things.

I update my blog when I get home from hanging out with Harry, before I do my tedious PT session on the bed.

I chew my pen and think carefully about the words I am going to use. I mean — what if Mom saw my blog? Not that she ever would. But just in case, I just write this:

Hi, it's Amelie here. I don't really have an update about the competition because like I said before, Mom has made it clear that I can't go to New York because it would be bad for my health.

And because I know she's right, I should probably listen to her . . . probably . . .

I leave it at that. When I log on again an hour later, there's a reply from a girl called Jen. It says:

Woo-hoo, girl! I'm sensing a cake rebellion. Keep us posted! My chocolate lava cake sank like a stone, so I won't put a picture of it here.

— Jen

Somewhere deep inside me, a little voice is telling me that I'm setting myself up for a disaster by acting like there is nothing wrong with me, but I choose to ignore it.

Mom is glad to see me being so much more energetic, but when she thinks I'm not looking, I catch her giving me puzzled glances and then almost saying something but thinking better of it.

By the end of the week, she has obviously decided she can't keep it to herself any longer.

We're sitting in front of the TV, devouring a plate of my strawberry-banana muffins and watching a sitcom we both like. When a commercial comes on, Mom leans forward and clicks the mute button on the remote.

"Amelie," she says, turning to me with a frown. She's wearing a fluffy pink robe and slippers, and her hair is up in a towel. Mom always has Bath Night on Friday when she gets home from work.

"What?" I say. I haven't really been concentrating on the show. My head is a blur of ideas, plans, and a good amount of devious lies that I am going to have to tell pretty soon.

"Well," says Mom. "I just wondered if there's anything going on that you're not telling me about? Because since the checkup, you've been kind of jumpy and restless, and although you're eating and sleeping and looking better, I'm wondering if it's a little bit of an act?"

The show comes back on, and I make a move for the remote, but Mom grabs it first and puts it under her bottom.

"Health is more important," she says. "So? I'm waiting."

A whole wave of conflicting thoughts is crashing around in my head. Part of me badly wants to tell Mom. Even though she drives me up the wall sometimes, she's still the person who is most on my side in the whole world, more than even Harry. He doesn't see me at my worst, when I'm really sick and hooked up to machines and yelling at Mom out of misery and frustration. Mom has seen it all for years and years, and she is still here caring for me.

But if I tell her, she will morph into the "CF Police" again, and my plan will be trampled into the mud.

I stall for a little bit by reaching for another muffin and dissecting it into soft lumps on my plate. I used giant, moist strawberries and bananas just at the peak of their ripeness, along with a bunch of butter and sugar from Karim's store. I managed to work two hours after school last night and didn't need to sit down once to catch my breath.

"Amelie," she says. "Will you just tell me what's going on, for goodness' sake? I wouldn't mind going to bed before midnight."

Uh-oh. Mom getting sarcastic is never a good sign. It's usually followed by a flare-up of anger and slamming doors.

I stretch and give her my best smile. "Nothing is going on," I say. "I'm just happy. I'm back together with Harry, and I feel a little better. I'm allowed to be happy, aren't I?"

Mom's face softens. She reaches out and touches my hair. "Of course, sweetheart," she says. "I just want you to know that you can always talk to me about, you know, the way that CF makes you feel. Okay?"

"Okay," I say, eating the last few crumbs of muffin and slurping down my hot chocolate. Mom put a swirl of whipped cream and some chocolate flakes on top just to get in as many calories as possible.

"Night," says Mom, getting up. "Oh — have you had your Creon? And done your breathing?"

I give a deep, impatient sigh. "Yeah, yeah," I say. "I don't want Tom to give me another lecture."

Mom smiles and flicks off the kitchen light. "Oh — and Amelie," she says as she starts going upstairs. "Don't forget that we're going to the hospital on Monday for you to have your gastrostomy fitted. I told the school that you'll be out for a couple of days."

"Okey dokey, artichokey," I say. Then I wonder why I said that. I sound like I'm ninety. It's hard to get Mom off my case sometimes.

I go upstairs to my room and shut the door. Then I grab the piggy bank off my dresser and plop down in the middle of my bed. I take the top off the piggy bank and dump out all the money in front of me. My whole life, I've kept the promise not to use this money for anything without first getting Mom's permission. I feel a little guilty, but it's the only way I can pull off my plan.

"Wow," I say after I've counted up all the money. There's close to fifteen hundred dollars. I've been filling this piggy bank with my allowances, Christmas gifts, and birthday gifts from relatives since I can remember. Unlike most girls my age, I hardly ever buy clothes or makeup, and I get most of my baking ingredients from Karim, so I don't need to buy things often.

"Well, good," I say to myself. "That should cover everything."

I get under the covers, but it's hot and I'm too excited to sleep, so after a while I get up again and find a book, but I can't even concentrate on that.

In the end I just lie on top of the covers, staring up at the white ceiling and going through recipes in my head. I must have fallen asleep, because I wake up in the same position six hours later, and it's Saturday.

Mornings are not good when you have CF. All the gunk in your chest seems to get harder and thicker overnight, and you wake up with a heavy, clogged feeling that's difficult to shake.

I stay in bed and do my breathing cycle for forty minutes until I've pushed tons of mucus up out of my airways. When I first started doing the PT myself, forty minutes felt like a lifetime to be trapped on a bed without getting up, but now I hardly notice. Then I rest for five minutes, swing my legs over the side of the bed, and get dressed in my leggings, a white tank top, and silver ballet flats. I brush my long, dark hair and let it fall over my shoulders. I study my face in the mirror. I'm always pale because of my CF, but today there's a tiny flush of color in my cheeks.

I'm meeting Jenna in town, and I'm going to tell her my secret.

It's a big one.

And I need her help.

***

"You're crazy," says Jenna.

We're sitting in McDonald's and munching on burgers and fries. I have two cheeseburgers and a large side of fries and a strawberry milk shake. Jenna has some weird chicken sandwich and a small portion of fries.

I click the plastic lid off my milk shake and stir the thick goop around with my red straw. "I'm not crazy," I say. "I'm just ambitious. I need to do this. I want to live my life — what's left of it."

Jenna screws up her face and nibbles on the end of a fry. "Your mom is going to kill you when she finds out anyway," she says. "So I don't think you'll need to worry about CF shortening your life any longer."

"Ha, ha," I say, but my determined smile is fading. I've been trying not to picture Mom's face when she finds out. I can't afford to think about it. If I do, I'll be swamped with horrible guilt and have to call the whole thing off. Besides, it's too late now. I've gone so far with the planning that I couldn't go back now even if I wanted to.

"What do you want me to do?" asks Jenna. "Because I'm not so sure I should be backing you up on this. What if you get really sick and there's nobody to help you? Maybe I should come with you."

I pull a piece of slimy lettuce off of my burger and sigh. If I were making this same meal at home, I would have made the burger out of lean beef and shaped it into a thick, juicy patty. I would have served it on a homemade bun with heaps of fresh heirloom tomatoes and tons of good Dijon mustard.

"Never mind the burger," says Jenna, reading my mind. She knows me so well. "Do you want me to come with you?"

I put down my burger and switch to the fries instead. They're okay, I guess, but they don't really taste like potato, just fat and salt. Still, it's all calories. I shovel them in and give Jenna my best smile.

"That's really nice of you," I say. "But then my mother will kill you, too, or probably your own mother will kill you.

So there would be two tragic deaths. Maybe we should just keep it to one."

I expect Jenna to laugh, but she looks mournful and pushes the remains of her meal in my direction. "I wish you didn't have CF," she says. "It sucks."

"You're telling me," I say, biting into her chicken sandwich and making a face at the dry, stringy chicken inside the bun. "But there's not much I can do about that. Except I really, really want to do this. And I need you to pretend that I'm coming over to your house on Sunday afternoon to do homework and then have dinner. Okay?"

Jenna nods. "Okay," she says. "But when your mom realizes you're gone, she's going to call me, isn't she? What do I say then?"

"I'm leaving her a note," I say. "Just tell her to read it. And tell her it was me who made you go along with the plan. She won't be angry with you then. I just need to get to New York before she knows, that's all."

Jenna sighs and finishes off her fries. "Are you going to tell Harry?" she asks. "Maybe he could go with you."

I've already thought about that. "I don't think I can tell him," I say. "I think he would side with Mom. Say I wasn't up for it."

Jenna nods. She knows how protective Harry can be. The three of us have a lot of fun when we hang out, but she sees Harry watching my face for signs of tiredness and checking to make sure I've taken my pills, even though he doesn't do it in such an obvious way as Mom.

"You're kind of a nightmare, Amelie Day," she says. "You and your Flour Power."

I grin at her. "I need to buy another new dress," I say. "Come on. You're good at that."

We leave, arm in arm, and head to the mall.

I spend two hours trying on different dresses in different stores, and Jenna and I can't agree on which ones look good and which ones don't. But in the end, we both agree on a white sundress with a brown cut-off cardigan over the top and a pair of brown flats with little leather flowers on them.

"It looks good, but you also won't fall over in it," says Jenna as I get out my wad of cash and pay for the things. "And you'll probably have an apron over the whole thing anyway, won't you?"

"I guess so," I say. I sit down and cough. My newfound energy is starting to wane a little, and I feel a small pang of fear in my stomach. Now that I have the outfit, it feels like this is really going to happen. And I don't know what to expect at all, other than that I have to be there on Monday at nine-thirty in the morning.

And that I'm traveling to New York City alone.

CHAPTER 11

On Sunday morning, Dad comes over to see me.

"I really hope it goes well tomorrow, Mel," he says. We're sitting outside in our courtyard garden where horses used to tread. Sometimes it's weird thinking that I live in a building where horses were tied up and taken out to hook up to old carriages. Once or twice at night, I swear I've heard the neigh of a horse and the stamping of hooves, but I'm probably just imagining it.

"What?" I say with a start. I'm half asleep today. I couldn't sleep at all last night from mulling it all over in my head. For a second I think that he's figured it out — my plan. Then I realize that he's referring to my operation. I wish I could tell Dad where I'm really going. I know that he wants me to follow my heart and my cooking and try to fulfill all my ambitions while I've still got enough breath to do it. I also know that he'd be very angry if I did something behind Mom's back.

That's why I can't risk telling him.

"Oh, thanks," I say in what I hope is a vague way. I need to change the subject. Quick.

"I made mixed berry tarts," I say. "Mini ones. Do you want some?"

Dad stretches out on his chair in the sun and makes a noise of satisfaction.

"Now you're talking," he says. "What are you waiting for? Bring on the cake!"

I go inside to put a tray together. Mom is in the kitchen watering all her houseplants. The sight of her back and the way that she's humming as she waters make guilty tears threaten to spring up in my eyes. For a moment I feel really small. Then I have a feeling of genuine fear. This is my home, the place where I feel safe, where Mom looks after me. And I'm going to remove myself from my safety zone and throw myself into the Great Unknown, all on my own.

"They look nice," says Mom, turning around and watching me put the mini tarts onto a big white plate. I've put strips of crisscrossed pastry across the glistening red tops of each little tart. "Save me one. I'll be out in a minute. Oh — maybe we can take the rest to the hospital tomorrow, for after the operation? I know how you hate hospital food."

"Mm hmm," I say, ducking out through the back door into the courtyard.

Dad bites into my crumbly pastry and gooey berry mixture with an exclamation of bliss.

"You really are good at this, aren't you?" he says, letting

crumbs fall all over his blue shirt. "It's a shame you can't go to that competition. You would've done really well."

He rolls up his sleeves and lies back in the sun with his eyes closed. I dissect the strips of pastry from the top of my tart and suck on them, but I'm not really thinking about the recipe for once. All I can think about is what I have to do later.

I hope that it works.

***

I do my breathing after Dad's gone, and then I make sure that my pillbox has everything I'm going to need in it. I drag out my duffel bag from under my bed and I pack the pillbox, the inhaler, the nebulizer, and a plastic bowl in case I need to throw up. The oxygen tank is too big and bulky for me to manage, so I leave it at home.

I feel sick already, but it's probably just nerves.

I put the new dress, cardigan, and shoes in my duffel, along with the gray tunic that Mom bought me and pack a pair of leggings, a pair of jeans, and a couple of tank tops and T-shirts. Then I put in a water bottle and several bags of chips and bars of chocolate. At the top, I put a couple of my mixed berry tarts in a plastic container, and on top of that I put my pink leather wallet stuffed to the brim with money.

Then I zip it up with some effort and stuff the duffel bag under my bed.

I'm done just in time. Mom comes in without knocking.

"Is Jenna's mom feeding you tonight?" she asks. "Or will you be back for dinner?"

"Feeding me," I say. It's scary how good I'm getting at this lying business.

Mom smiles. "It's grilled cheese and *Dancing with the Stars* for me, then," she says. "Hooray."

I wait until I hear her go into the bathroom, and then I sneak downstairs with my duffel bag and go out to the front yard. I hide the bag behind the green recycling bin and come back inside.

Mom comes downstairs with a pile of laundry in her arms. "Are you heading out?" she says. "Don't be late coming home. Remember, we need to be up early for the hospital tomorrow."

"Yeah, I just need to get my stuff," I say, bolting upstairs again. I go to Mom's room and creep over to the bed. I pull a letter out of my wallet and put it on her pillow. Then I cover the pillow a little with her comforter and creep out again.

I pick up a black leather purse from my room and grab a couple of my schoolbooks, which I hold under my arm so that Mom can see them.

Then I go downstairs to say goodbye.

Mom gives me a big kiss. "You're being very brave about tomorrow," she says. "You must be kind of nervous. I know I am."

I feel a big pang in my chest. I don't like lying to Mom. Then again, I wouldn't know how to stop this now. It has gone too far.

I take a quick look at the cozy living room, at the cream-colored couch where I lie when I'm not feeling well, at the TV that I spend so many hours staring at, and then over Mom's shoulder to the kitchen where all my pans and trays and ingredients live.

A pang of something horrible comes up into my throat, and for once it's not mucus.

I force a smile. "See you later, Mom," I say.

Then I go outside to the front yard, grab my duffel bag from behind the recycling bin, leave my schoolbooks there, and head off down the road.

CHAPTER 12

I walk to the train station in town.

It takes about twenty minutes, and the whole time I'm looking around to see if any of Mom's friends or neighbors are about to drive past and notice me, but they don't.

It's a steep walk up the hill as the road nears the station. I feel the familiar tightness in my chest, so I sit down on a bench for a moment and catch my breath, take a deep puff on my inhaler. Then I hoist the duffel bag onto my shoulder again, cross the busy main road, and go inside the station.

The station is small, and there aren't many people around on Sunday afternoon. I approach the ticket office feeling like I'm on a secret spy mission or something.

"One ticket to New York City, please," I say, dropping the duffel bag to the ground. I forgot how heavy it was going to be with all my medicine in it. At the last moment I put in some little bottles of high-calorie protein shakes, but they're really weighing me down.

"One-way or round-trip?" says the guy behind the counter.

I consider this for a moment. "Don't know yet," I say. It all depends on whether I bomb at the first stage of the quarterfinals on Monday or whether I go through to the semifinals, which are being filmed on Wednesday. "One-way, I guess."

"That'll be seventy-six dollars," says the guy.

I nearly pass out when he says this. Seventy-six dollars!

"Is there a cheaper ticket?" I say. "That's kind of a lot."

The man laughs. "When did you last go to New York?" he asks. "That's the standard off-peak rate. It costs more than that on weekdays, especially during rush hour."

I flush. I haven't been on the train to New York for at least a year, and last time Mom was with me and bought the tickets.

I shove my cash in his direction. A little orange ticket whizzes out of a machine, and he slides it under the glass toward me. I put the ticket in the front of my wallet, and then I hoist up the duffel bag again and go to wait at the platform.

I've got five minutes until the train comes. I take out a bottle of protein shake and drink it while I'm waiting. Then I start on a bag of chips.

The train pulls in, and I heave my duffel onto it and find a seat. As soon as I sit down, a great wave of tiredness and relief comes over me. I've done it. I'm actually on the train to New York City.

The train car is pretty empty, so I get all my food out and arrange it around me. I take my Creon and then eat a sandwich that I made this morning while Mom wasn't looking. I finish up with a Milky Way and then put the food away in the duffel bag. Then I put all my medical stuff into my small black leather bag so that I've got it all together, and I put it on the seat next to me. I prop up my feet on the duffel and get out my list of recipe notes so that I can start rehearsing how to bake them in my head.

The train lurches and sways through the Pennsylvania countryside. It's very hot, and I feel exhausted. I lean my head against the window for a moment and watch all the trees and fields whiz by in a blur. I don't suppose it matters if I take a short nap. I'm going to need all my energy for what lies ahead.

***

The next thing I know, I'm jolting awake with my head banging on the glass and a gross dry feeling in my mouth.

It takes me a while to remember where I am. My head is aching and my chest feels tight. It's like the past few days of plotting and planning kept me going. Now that the excitement of being secretive is gone, I feel like I've been in a fight. And lost.

I yawn and look at my watch. I must have been asleep for over two hours, because there's only a half an hour left until the train gets in to New York City. I take a little mirror out from the top pocket of my duffel bag and then attempt to tame my hair. My face looks thin and pale in the late afternoon sunlight, but I try to ignore that. I get a bottle of water out and another snack and then turn to get my black leather bag full of medicine so that I can take some more Creon.

It's gone.

Now I'm wide awake.

I search under the seat, behind the seat, and on all the other empty seats around me. Then I open my duffel just in case I'm going crazy and put the little black bag back in there without thinking, but it's not there either.

My heart pounds with fright and uncertainty. I don't know what to do now.

I check in my duffel for my phone and money, and they're still there, at least. Thank goodness I didn't put them in the leather bag. But who can I call? Mom isn't supposed to know where I am yet, and my train is about to arrive at Penn Station. I don't know a single soul in New York.

I try to think, even though tears are rising up and threatening to spill over.

Maybe I could find a pharmacy in the city and tell them I lost my drugs? But then they'd have to contact my doctor, and the doctor, in turn, would have to contact Mom, and then the game would be up.

I could call Jenna, but I couldn't expect her to sneak into my house, go upstairs to my bedroom, get all my spare medicine, sneak out, and then come all the way to New

York. And anyway, I don't want to turn my phone on in case Mom or Harry call and then my voice will sound guilty and give my scheme away.

I'm shivering even though the train is stuffy and the air conditioning isn't working. This so wasn't supposed to happen. I'm angry with myself for leaving the little bag on the seat beside me and then falling asleep. Somebody must have thought it contained money. That must be why they took it.

I sit there swearing and cursing and thinking, but I can't come up with any good solution.

No.

I'm going to have to try to get through the next few days without my meds.

I've never had to do that before. If I eat meals without Creon, I get the worst stomachaches ever. If I get out of breath and have no inhaler, I might faint or choke.

Or die.

I feel really scared now.

I cling to my duffel bag.

The train grinds into Penn Station and comes to a screeching halt.

CHAPTER 13

I'd forgotten how busy New York City is.

Once I've dragged my duffel bag off the train and got it back onto my aching shoulder, I stand on the platform disoriented and dizzy as people rush past me and bang into my back and sides. They're like a swarm of ants all trying to run in different directions.

All I want to do is get to the hotel and draw the curtains, lie on the bed, and cry.

But first I have to figure out the subway.

I get on the escalator and rest my duffel bag on the railing beside me, but it sticks out and nearly trips up the people who are trying to rush down the other side. I lift it up and try to hold it in front of me, but my chest is hurting and I'm struggling to breathe. At the foot of the escalator, I have to stop to put it on my shoulder again, and a bunch of people behind me are in such a rush, they almost catapult over my head.

"Great place to stop, you stupid girl," says a woman in high heels. She clicks off, swinging her purse and shaking her head in annoyance.

I fight back tears. I would give anything to see a friendly face — Mom, Harry, even any kid from school — but that's not really likely here in the smelly bowels of the New York City train system, so after a quick look at the directions I printed off earlier, I drag myself across the huge station and then follow the signs to the 7th Avenue subway line.

Dazed, I walk toward the turnstile. My duffel gets caught in the automatic gates, and I have to go back and try again. But again, my duffel gets stuck.

A man behind me sighs in annoyance and gestures in the direction of the ticket attendant standing at a booth. "He'll let you through," he says.

I push my way through the crowd to the booth. Everybody else seems to be shoving and barging in, so I decide I might as well join in. I get a lot of rude remarks and glares from the people I'm hitting with my duffel, but I'm beyond caring.

Once I get through the gate by the ticket attendant, I find the #1 train. It is packed to the brim with people, even though it's Sunday evening. Most of them look like tourists. They have big backpacks or are staring at the map of the subway above my head and shouting at one another in loud voices of all different languages. Everyone is bleary-eyed and trying not to look at one another. The train shakes, stops, starts, and creaks endlessly.

I stand with my hand on the greasy pole in the middle

of the car and try not to panic. Mom has always told me to avoid public transportation because it's a hotbed of germs and viruses, and with CF I spend most of my time trying not to catch anything. We used to live in New York City, but Mom decided to move when she and Dad broke up. Her main reason was because of the increased risk of infection.

I push my way off when I get to Christopher Street/Sheridan Square. My hotel is in a part of Manhattan called Greenwich Village. I chose it on the Internet because it looked close to the studio where the baking competition is going to be filmed. I thought that Greenwich Village sounded cool — kind of pretty and artsy and hip.

Yeah, right.

The air is humid and stale-smelling, and I'm having some trouble breathing. I slide my duffel off my shoulders to give them a rest. Then I look left and right and consult the map I printed off this morning. The roads are crammed with traffic and people and I can't see the street names at first, so I set off in what I hope is the right direction. After about five minutes of struggle, I end up at a small concrete building that sits at one end of a square with railings around it. There's a flight of steps leading to the front door. I just can't face them right now, and there is still a bit of daylight left, so I cross the street and go find a bench in the square.

There's a statue of a woman's head next to where I'm sitting. She has a beaky nose and a thin, sad-looking face. The head is made of bronze and is covered in pigeon droppings. She looks about as miserable as I feel. I wonder if she had CF.

I sit next to the woman, lean back, and drink a ton of water from one of my bottles. I feel like I need a snack, but I'm scared to eat too much without my Creon, so I nibble on the corner of a Hershey's Bar and then fold the wrapper back over the rest and put it away again.

As the sunlight starts to fade, I drag myself back across the street and up the stairs into the hotel lobby.

The building is very modern. When I booked it, I'd pictured an old-fashioned colonial sort of building, with antique furniture in the lobby and a friendly woman at reception with maybe a hotel cat perched on the desk.

There's nobody at the small reception desk inside the door, so I ring the bell and wait.

A dark-haired woman with olive skin and large gold earrings shuffles down the hallway in a pair of oversized fluffy slippers.

"Yes, ma'am?" she says.

"I have a reservation here for three nights," I say, breathless. "I think."

"You look very young," says the woman.

"I'm eighteen," I lie, straightening up as tall as my short body will allow. I put my wallet on the desk and raise my eyebrows at her, tapping my fingertips on the polished wood in what I hope is a grown-up, impatient fashion.

"I have a room booked," I say again. "Melanie Smith." It's all part of my mega-plan of deception. I don't want anybody calling this hotel and somehow finding out that I'm here. Or at least — I didn't. None of this seems like such a good idea now that I've lost all my medication.

My chest is making noises that mean any moment now, I'm going to start to cough and not be able to stop.

The woman gives me a small smile. I bet I look pretty pale and washed up. "That comes to seven hundred and eighty dollars and sixteen cents," she says.

It's a lot of money, but I knew what the price would be ahead of time since I booked the room online. I take out my pink wallet and pull out seven one-hundred dollar bills, eight tens, and a one, and I hand it to her and then look down at the floor.

I can feel her eyes on me while she counts the cash. It's probably not often that guests pay in cash, but what choice did I have?

"You're checked in," she finally says, handing the change to me. "Continental breakfast is from eight to ten." Then the woman hands me a key and tells me that my room is on the second floor.

There's no elevator, so I drag myself up the stairs, my lungs aching with every step. I open the door to my room, shut it behind me, and look around. The room is very small. The double bed with its dull brown bedspread pretty much fills most of it. There is a tiny television on a table in one corner and a rickety desk with a little coffeemaker on top of it against the wall closest to the door. A white door leads into the smallest bathroom I have ever seen. There's no room for a bath, just a shower in the corner that's still dripping. On the shelf over the toilet are three tiny plastic bottles — shampoo, conditioner, and shower gel.

I stare around me at this dismal picture for a moment or two and try not to picture my pretty bedroom at home with its white soft sheets, oak desk, and bedside lamp. Then I unzip my duffel.

"Might as well unpack," I say, though there's nobody to say it to. I hang up my new dress in the cramped closet and put my T-shirts and jeans on a shelf inside it. Then I arrange all my snacks and drinks on the little table by the bed.

"Too bad I won't be able to eat you," I say to them. My stomach is growling with hunger and anxiety all at once.

I get my recipe notebook out and perch cross-legged on the bed, with my hair half falling in front of my face. I run through what I have to do a couple of times until I feel more confident. I had to email the television studio about two weeks ago with a list of all the ingredients I'm going to use, and I'm hoping that they were able to get everything I need.

At ten o'clock, I stop and lie down. My chest feels tight and clogged, and I'm missing my inhaler already. I look at my phone but can't bring myself to turn it on. Right about now, Mom will be calling Jenna to ask why I'm not back yet, because we've got to go to the hospital in the morning. And Jenna will have to confess her part in all this and tell Mom to go read the note on her pillow.

I feel sick when I think of Mom reading that note.

"Breathing," I say to myself. "At least I can still do that."

I lie on my back and do forty minutes of the autogenic drainage exercises like Tom showed me. The rattling in my chest is awful today. I don't think that CF reacts very well to stress.

After I finish my exercises, I eat a couple of cookies and eye the berry tarts that I made yesterday. They look good even cold, but I know if I eat too much without Creon, I'm going to be in agony in the middle of the night. I eat one bite from one of the tarts and then wrap it up again. I drink another high-calorie protein shake from one of my little bottles, and then I get into my pajamas and huddle under the thin blankets, with the cheap curtains doing a bad job of blocking out the city lights.

Down below my room, the city continues to roar with life right into the next morning. The traffic in the square honks and roars and brakes squeal. About a million fire trucks zoom past with their sirens blaring every half hour or so through the night.

At three in the morning, I get up and drink some water. My stomach feels tender when I press it, and I'm struggling a little for breath. I sit by the window and gaze down on the lights of New York until I feel tired. Then I hop back into bed and at last fall asleep not long before it's time to get up.

**

When I get up in the morning light, I do my breathing again. I turn on the small coffeemaker and make myself a cup of coffee with sugar to try to make up for the lack of sleep.

I get out my best red T-shirt and skinny jeans and lay them on the bed while I take a shower. The water only seems to come out lukewarm, but I don't really have any other option, so I rinse off as best I can and use the hotel conditioner on my hair because I left my own bottle at home.

The whole time I'm getting ready, I hum loudly. I'm trying to block out the thoughts of Mom that keep popping into my head. She will be furious. And worried out of her mind. And embarrassed because she'll have to call the hospital and tell them that I won't be coming in for my operation after all.

At least she won't be able to find my hotel. I didn't even tell Jenna where I was staying. And I hid the letter with the details of the competition in hopes that Mom won't remember where it is taking place.

I make a face at myself in the mirror. I look dreadful. My skin is white and dry, and there are dark circles under my eyes. My hair is lank from the cheap conditioner, and I swear my face looks thinner than it did yesterday. I wish I could eat.

I wish I hadn't lost my purse on the train.

I manage to eat a few squares of dark chocolate with my coffee. That will have to do for breakfast. I have to get to the studio by nine-thirty, and it's already almost nine.

I put on a light jacket and stuff my pink wallet, phone, and recipe lists into one of my pockets, and two bottles of protein shakes into the other. I don't have a small bag to carry my stuff in, and I don't really want to turn up at the competition with that huge duffel bag, so it'll have to do.

I take a last look around the sad little room and leave it with relief. I take the elevator downstairs, go past reception, and step out into the bewildering mess and noise of Greenwich Village. I search around a little and find a line of yellow taxis, so I get into one, trying to look like I know what I'm doing, and I give the driver the address of the studios. Then I sit back and attempt to look like a healthy, confident, and streetwise New York City girl who hops into cabs every single day. I see the driver look at me once or twice in the mirror, and I know that this is not what he's seeing, but I keep a silly smile on my face and look at the streets with what I hope is a knowing sort of look.

The cab ride costs over fifteen dollars, which seems like a lot for such a short ride, but I pay it with the same smile on my face and then turn around and prance into the building in front of me like I've known it all my life.

I find myself standing in a huge glass-walled lobby with a shiny black desk right at the very end of it. There's a woman sitting behind it, so I go and give her my name. She writes my name on a plastic badge and tells me to put it on and wait on the black couches. I sink into the soft black leather and gaze up at the giant TVs in front of me. A bunch of trendy-looking people rush into the lobby and flash their security passes at a machine to get into the main building.

I sit with my legs crossed, chewing my lip and looking around. I hope they don't forget about me. I'm finding it hard to believe I made it to New York all on my own, spent a night in a gloomy hotel, and then found my way here.

"This is it," I whisper to myself for confidence. "Flour Power!"

I feel a little better when I think of my favorite catchphrase, but not for long. There's the familiar, dreaded shifting in the center of my chest and the feeling of something catching.

"Oh no," I mutter. Then I double up with my head toward my knees and cough like there's no tomorrow. The noise echoes around the polished lobby and seems to bounce off the walls and come back to me, like a cough boomerang. People stare at me as they walk past, but nobody stops.

I cough on and on. Can't seem to stop. I could use my inhaler right now and a nice steadying breath of oxygen.

When I come up for air, there's a woman standing over me with a look of concern on her face. "Are you all right?" she says. "You don't look too good."

She's tall with blond hair and has a name badge on that says, "Elaine McDonald, Floor Manager."

I glance at the shiny floors around us. "Your floors look very well managed," I say, trying to be polite, even though I'm finding it hard to catch my breath.

The woman stares at me for a moment. Then she sees me looking at her nametag and bursts out laughing. "Well," she says, "actually I'm the floor manager in the studio. It means that I direct everybody when the cameras are rolling. Make sure everyone is in the right place. Anyway, are you here for *Best Teen Baker*? Don't you have a parent with you?"

I nod. My eyes are watering from the last bout of coughing, but I stand up and shake the woman's hand. "Nice to meet you," I say. "Sorry. I just got over the flu. And my mom is coming later."

Wow. I could lie for the Olympic Games, I'm getting so good at it, I think as I follow Elaine into the black elevators at the back of the building, and she takes me down endless corridors and up more flights of stairs until I'm gasping for air again, but I do my best to hide it. We end up in a big space full of cooking stations and people setting up cameras and microphones.

"Here we are," says Elaine. "We'll have rehearsal when everybody's here. That means you'll get to run through your recipes before the cameras start rolling. Okay?"

I nod. That sounds like a good idea. I'm so tired and nervous that my brain has gone blank. I finger the recipe book in my pocket for comfort.

"The main competition will be filmed at four," says Elaine. "It won't be broadcast on TV for another few months. You'll have to sign an agreement not to tell anybody about what happens, so the viewers keep watching to find out."

I nod again. I like Elaine. She seems friendly and smart. If only she also doubled as a CF nurse and I could tell her that I desperately need some oxygen. I catch a glimpse of my reflection in the shiny door of the giant fridge on set, and I swear that my lips are actually turning a little blue around the edges.

"Can I get you something to drink?" Elaine is saying. "It's so hot outside. Great air-conditioning in here, though."

In fact, I feel frozen. Because I'm thinner than a girl my age should be, I feel cold even in the middle of summer. The air-conditioning in here is sharp and vicious, blowing great gusty drafts of ice-cold air around my aching bones.

"Something warm would be good," I say. Elaine sends another girl off with orders for a couple of coffees and then she is distracted by the arrival of another group of competitors, so I take the chance to sit on a stool and steady myself.

I take a look at the cooking stations. They're really cool. There are twelve of them spread around the large studio, each with a built-in stove and plenty of granite work surface for chopping and food preparation. Shiny steel spotlights are angled over each station, and as I look around, a man comes in with a huge cart and starts unloading ingredients. I recognize mine when he starts putting out a bunch of dark chocolate bars and sugar for my mini chocolate lava cakes, dark brown sugar and molasses for my sticky gingerbread, and boxes of eggs and cartons of cream for my Chantilly crème and vanilla custard. Then he puts out flour, cocoa powder, chopped nuts, and butter for my almond macaroons.

My heart beats a little faster from all the excitement and nerves. I made it. I'm here. I'm actually going to take part in the competition!

That's if my chest doesn't seize up first. It really hurts.

I'm trying to ignore the pain, but I'm wondering if I have another chest infection, because I feel a little dizzy and, although I'm shivering, my head is burning hot. I've lost my appetite, too. Even the thought of a cookie makes me feel sick.

I gulp the hot, sugary cappuccino that Elaine's assistant brings me and lick the froth off my lips. It's not as good as the ones I make at home, but I feel a little better, even though my stomach feels twisted and tender.

I wonder who it was who stole my purse. I bet they were awfully disappointed when they opened it and found a bunch of useless pills and medical gadgets, rather than a big wallet full of money or an expensive iPhone.

"Serves them right," I mutter.

Then we're all beckoned over to the cooking stations where our ingredients are piled.

I take a look at the other contestants. There are five other girls and six boys, most of them about the same age as me, although there are some who look older. The girls look very assured and confident. They're all in jeans and pretty tops with shiny hair tied back in fluffy ponytails and tons of lip gloss.

I hadn't thought to put any makeup on for today.

My T-shirt is plain and red and boring. I was saving the best outfit for if I made it to the final. I tug at my hair and try to let it fall over my face in what I hope passes for a sophisticated and confident manner, but it just lies in lank strands over my shoulders.

I'm wondering whether I should make the effort to go talk with the other contestants, when Elaine bears down on me in a cloud of sickly perfume. Great. Another cough trigger.

"You'll have to tie that up," she whispers, pointing at my hair and passing me an elastic band. "Food hygiene."

I gather up my hair and pull it back into a thin ponytail. I hate having my hair tied back, so now I feel like my pale, ill face is even more on show than it was before.

A bunch of new lights come on. They're so bright that I almost can't see for a moment. "Okay, folks," shouts a man behind a camera with a clapboard in his hand. "We're doing a practice run to see how you all look and to get you used to this cooking equipment. Just relax and cook your best recipes. You have two hours."

Elaine is standing next to him with a clipboard in her hand. She gives us all the thumbs-up, and the man shouts, "And . . .

ACTION!" Before I know it, I'm deep into measuring out flour and melting butter and molasses for my German gingerbread.

I lose myself in what I'm doing. It's amazing, cooking in the TV studio with all the beautiful pots and shiny equipment. I'm so immersed in the joy of it that I jump out of my skin when a buzzer sounds and the man behind the camera shouts, "And . . . CUT! Good job, everybody."

Elaine comes over and has a word with each of us in turn.

When she reaches my station, she smiles. "You did very well, especially if you're still recovering from the flu," she says. I know I must look pretty terrible, because I feel dreadful. "So what will happen later when we're filming is that the judges will call you forward with your three dishes, and they'll try a mouthful of each and tell you what they think. Then they'll decide who's going through to the semifinals. Okay?"

She's about to move on to the next contestant and say the same thing again, but I stop her. "Elaine," I say, "what happens now? We have a while until it's four o'clock."

"You're free," says Elaine. "You need to be back here at two-thirty for hair and makeup. Other than that, the afternoon is yours! Go and enjoy New York!"

I can't think of anything worse.

My heart sinks into my black ballet flats as I trudge out of the building and back into the hot, smelly streets of the city. I haven't eaten a decent meal in over twenty-four hours, and my head is throbbing.

I find a diner nearby and order a fried egg on toast and a cup of tea, but my throat seems to be closing up and diners never seem to be able to cook a fried egg the way I like it. When I make them at home, I use super-hot olive oil and cook the egg on high heat, spooning the oil over the white to avoid getting that gross jelly part around the yolk. I like the edges nice and frizzled and crispy and the yolk soft and hot. This egg is all wrong. The white is soggy and cold, and the yolk has turned to thick yellow rubber. I find it hard to shove the greasy food down my throat. Without Creon, it's not going to get digested properly anyway, so eventually I give up and just drink the tea.

I feel another major coughing session coming on, so I pay and leave the diner right away. Then I find a small square of green in the center of the busy streets and sit on a bench. I hack my guts up, rattling and retching and gasping for breath, and then everything starts to spin, so I clutch the edge of the bench and tell myself not to panic, but it's no good.

I'm really struggling for every breath now. I'm not sure how I'm going to even stand up straight, let alone get back to the TV studios and cook my three recipes again in front of the cameras for real this time.

I sit with my head buried in my hands, trying to think.

In the end I do the only thing I can think of doing.

The thing I didn't want to do at all.

I fumble in my pocket and take out my phone.

German Gingerbread with Vanilla Custard

For the gingerbread, you will need:

- 1 stick of butter
- 1 ¾ cups dark brown sugar
- 3 tablespoons water
- 3 tablespoons molasses
- 3 cups flour
- 2 eggs, beaten
- 1 ½ tablespoons ground ginger
- 1 tablespoon ground cinnamon
- A pinch of salt
- 1 teaspoon baking soda
- 1 cup warm milk

For the vanilla custard, you will need:

- ¾ cup milk
- 1 cup heavy cream
- 1 teaspoon vanilla extract

- ⅓ cup granulated sugar
- 2 free-range egg yolks (you can use non-free-range, but these do taste better and are much kinder to the hens)

Preheat the oven to 300°F. Grease and line a loaf pan (or an 11 ½ x 7 ½ inch cake pan) — you can line it with parchment paper, which is easily found in the supermarket.

Get a large saucepan and slowly melt the molasses, sugar, and butter together on a low heat. When the mixture is nice and gloopy, remove from the heat and stir in the beaten eggs. Sieve the flour, salt, cinnamon, and ginger into the melted mixture.

Sieve the baking soda into a mixing bowl and pour the warm milk over it. Add this to the molasses mixture, stirring well to combine all the ingredients. Pour into the pan and bake for about 90 minutes.

Allow the gingerbread to cool in the pan before removing.

If you like the top of your gingerbread to be extra messy and sticky and delicious — which, let's face it, I do, because I'm obsessed with this stuff — then brush some butter on the top while the cake is still warm.

To make the vanilla custard, place the milk, cream, and vanilla in a saucepan on low heat. Gently bring to a boil, then remove from the heat.

Whisk the sugar and egg yolks together in a large bowl with a hand whisk (or a fork if you don't have one) until pale and frothy. Pour the egg mixture over the milk and cream and whisk together. Pour the mixture into a clean saucepan and continue whisking over low heat until a frothy custard is formed. Then pour into a small pitcher and serve with a big, thick slice of the German gingerbread.

CHAPTER 14

Harry answers on the first ring. He usually never does that, so I know I'm in trouble.

"Mel!" he says. "Where are you? I've been trying to call you all morning."

I sigh and swallow down huge lumps of mucus in an effort to be able to talk to him. Just hearing his low, kind voice is making me want to burst out sobbing. "I'm in Greenwich Village," I whisper, but still trying to be heard above the roar of traffic. "I'm doing the competition."

"Yeah, I know," says Harry. "I didn't think you'd actually be stupid enough to go behind your mom's back. You do know that she's furious, right? And going out of her mind with worry?"

I sit up straight. "You talked to my mom?" I say to him. "Why?"

"Uh, why do you think?" says Harry. "You didn't come home last night. She thought you might be with me. Oh, and

130

she spoke to Jenna, too, and read your letter. So she knows exactly where you are."

"Well, not exactly," I mutter, blushing even though he can't see me. "She can't know exactly."

"Stop being an idiot," says Harry in a voice very unlike his normal mild one. "She's worried herself sick. You were supposed to be at the hospital now."

"I know," I whisper. "I just had to do this competition. You know how much it means to me."

"Well, yeah," says Harry. "I do. But maybe your mother should mean more to you?"

There's silence while I digest the horribleness of what I've done.

"Anyway," says Harry. "She's in kind of a bad state at home, and your dad's with her. So I suggested that I come up to New York and meet my aunt who lives there. We'll come get you, get some dinner, and then we can come home together on the train. The hospital says you can still be admitted tonight if you get a move on."

I scowl against the blinding light of the sun. I'm sitting on a bench that has no shade whatsoever. "I'm not coming home until I'm done with the competition," I tell him. "I'm here now, and I have already competed in the rehearsal. Hold on."

I cover the mouthpiece and bend over to cough.

When I've finished, there's a loud sigh from Harry on the other end of the line. "Are you taking your medication?" he asks. "You sound terrible."

"Thanks," I say feebly. I hang onto the phone like it's the last possession I'm ever going to have. I don't want to lose Harry's voice in my ear, even if he *is* upset with me.

"Have you had your pills today?" asks Harry. He's not going to give up.

I wait a moment to make sure that I really need to say what I'm about to say, but then I get dizzy again and everything spins around. "I lost the bag with my medicine in it," I say in a small voice. "On the train. So I haven't had anything since yesterday afternoon."

"Jeez, Mel!" says Harry. He sounds like he's going to burst a few major blood vessels. "Why didn't you call me? Or find a doctor? Or come home? Are you stupid or something?"

He's so angry that I melt into a puddle of insecurity and begin to cry. "I just wanted to prove that I could do something," I say between sobs. "I hate being the stupid girl with CF who can't do anything because she gets out of breath."

That's a silly thing to say, because now I'm so out of breath that I can't really talk.

"Okay, so you got to New York on your own," says Harry. "Big freakin' deal. Now you're in trouble, so I'm coming to get you. I promised your mom. Give me the name of the place you're staying."

He's not going to take any more argument from me. I can tell by the tone of his voice. Harry takes down the name and address of the hotel and the TV studio.

"Okay," he says. "I'm going to the station now. I'll go to your house first and get your meds. I should be there by two. Stay at the hotel and don't go anywhere, okay?"

"I need to be in hair and makeup at two-thirty," I say in a small protesting voice, but Harry makes a noise of disgust.

"Thanks, Harry," I say, but he has already hung up.

I sit on the bench, and the floodgates finally open.

I cry and cry and cry.

***

By the time it gets close to two, I feel calmer.

I've decided what I'm going to do. I'm going to call Harry and tell him — tell, not ask — that I am going to do the competition whether he likes it or not. Then if I don't do well, I will go home with him. But if I do well, we can both stay in New York — Harry with his aunt and me in this hotel — and I will call Mom and tell her that I'm okay, but that I won't be having the operation.

I'm back in my room, sitting on the bed. I've changed into a prettier top with flowers on it, but I'm wearing the same jeans. I bought a bottle of shampoo and washed my hair, even though it took me about ten times longer than usual because I had to keep stopping to lean against the shiny white tiles of the bathroom wall to catch my breath.

I put on a smear of pink lip gloss to cover up my blue lips and survey myself in the mirror. "Better," I say. Then I double over and cough until I throw up. The next time I look in the mirror, the lip gloss is smeared, and my mascara has made damp black marks down my cheeks. "Oh well," I say. "They're going to do my makeup anyway."

I glance at my watch. It's just about two o'clock now, and I have to get in a cab in the next five minutes or else I won't get to the studio in time.

Where's Harry?

I try his cell a couple of times, but it goes straight to voicemail. Then my phone rings while I'm holding it, and I nearly drop it in fright. "Mom" flashes up on the display, so immediately I turn the phone off in a panic and shove it back into my pocket. I can't handle Mom's anger right now. She is so going to give me the biggest, angriest lecture known to man. Or girl. And if Dad gets ahold of me, I'm going to be toast — and not the delicious, crunchy, white homemade kind either, but the thin black charred variety made using bland sliced bread.

When it's 2:15, I can't wait any longer.

I go downstairs as fast as I can and run outside to hail a cab. Running is not a good idea, but I can't be late for the quarterfinals of *Best Teen Baker*. I just can't.

***

At 2:30, I'm sitting in a white room full of gleaming mirrors and vases of red flowers. A lady named Chell, which I'm guessing might be short for Michelle, is puffing powder all over my face with a big soft brush.

"Anti-shine," she says. "Those TV lights can be very unforgiving. Although you do have amazing skin. Wish mine was as good."

That's the first nice thing anybody's said to me about my appearance in forever, and it makes me want to cry. Crying is not a great thing to do when you have CF, because the illness already gives you blocked sinuses, and crying screws up your breathing. I've already done too much crying today, so I wait until I'm sure my voice isn't going to wobble, and then I thank her.

"Sure I can't get you another drink, hon?" she says, spraying my hair with some gross chemical-smelling stuff. I squeeze my lips shut and try not to breathe any of it in. Everything in this makeup room is a potential cough hazard. "I hear you had the flu."

I give her a weak smile and nod my head. If only I did have the flu. If I had the flu, it would go away in a few days and then I'd be healthy. If I had the flu, my worried boyfriend wouldn't be on a train coming to get me, and my mother wouldn't be on the warpath of anxiety and rage.

"You do look a little pale," Chell says, considering my face. "Just a little more blush, don't you think?"

Actually, I don't think. I look like I've been boiled in beet juice. But she adds a little more color to my cheekbones and stands back to survey her handiwork.

"There," she says. "We've done a good job of putting some color back on you!"

I snort and then try to cover it up by blowing my nose. If only she and everyone here knew the true story behind my pale complexion. Probably just as well they don't, or else I'd be in a New York hospital bed right now and not about to enter the competition I've been waiting to get to for so long.

Underneath my excitement and nerves, I feel so ill that I think I might just keel over and die at any point, but I'm determined to bake my lava cakes, my gingerbread, and my cookies and wow the judges with them first. Then at least I could die happy. Or part-happy — because actually I really want to move on to the semifinals, too.

"Is there anybody waiting for me in reception?" I ask Chell. "My boyfriend is supposed to be coming."

Chell sends another girl down to reception to look, but she comes back and shakes her head.

"Oh well," I say. "He must have gotten stuck on a train somewhere."

I feel disappointed and relieved at the same time. I could do without him giving me a major lecture, but then again, he has all my meds and I needed them like . . . yesterday.

And if I saw Harry here, I know I'd bake the best I've ever baked.

Just to make him proud of me again.

***

We're standing behind our cooking stations primed for action.

The cameras begin to roll, and the host of the show steps forward. He's a large man with a polished bald head and glasses, and he's wearing a gray pin-striped suit. He looks more like a used-car salesman than the host of a cooking show, but he has a big grin, and when we were all introduced to him just before the cameras began to roll, he took the trouble to talk a little with each of us.

With the camera pointing at him now, the man introduces the show and explains the competition. Then some dramatic music comes pounding into the studio and the man holds his breath for a moment, looks up at us where we're standing in our aprons behind our stoves, and then bellows out, "ONE, TWO, THREE — LET'S BAKE!"

My legs feel weak. I turn the oven on, grease my cake pan, grab my mixing bowl, and measure out the flour.

Okay. This is it. This is the day that will affect the rest of my life.

I start with the gingerbread, since it takes the longest to bake. I put butter and brown sugar in a big steel saucepan, stirring the mixture with a wooden spoon until it melts into a smooth brown puddle, and then I pour in the water and molasses. When it's all broken down into a thick, sticky mixture, I beat in a couple of large eggs. Then in the big mixing bowl next to me I put the flour, ground ginger, eggs, salt, and cinnamon and then tip it all into the glorious, gooey molasses mix. I stir and stir to make sure all the ingredients are mixed in, otherwise there will be uneven clumps of flour in the middle of the cake. The spicy, gingery, buttery smell is like heaven. Then I fold in warm milk mixed with baking soda until the texture changes from a sticky dark brown to pale, cappuccino-colored foam, which begins to rise up toward the rim of the saucepan. I taste a spoonful and nod. It's ready. I pick up the saucepan and tip the rich, frothy mixture into my prepared loaf pans, and then I slide them into the oven to bake for just under an hour.

Macaroons next. I line a baking sheet with edible rice paper, and then I mix together my sugar and ground almonds. I add some almond essence, just a pinch of salt, and an egg white and then beat the whole mixture until it's ready to be piped in little circles onto the rice paper.

I sprinkle powdered sugar over the unbaked cookies, and then add an almond to the top of each. I can't resist popping one into my mouth. Uh-oh. That was a dumb idea. Nuts are not a good snack to have when you are trying not to cough. I take a swig from my bottle of water and try to calm the choking feeling. Then I pop the macaroons into the oven for ten minutes. I wipe the sweat off my head with my right arm and make a mental note to trim the rice paper to fit each cookie when they're baked.

At last, I turn my attention to the lava cakes, the most risky of my three dishes. The right cooking time is essential to get the runny center inside the cake. If you cook them too long, they just become like regular chocolate cake instead.

I melt dark chocolate and butter together in a bowl over a saucepan of hot water. Then in a big brown mixing bowl, I beat my sugar, egg yolks, whole eggs, and flour together. I pour the melted chocolate mixture into this bowl and then fold in the flour with a large metal spoon. I scoop up a fingerful of the mixture and test it. It's sweet, but with a slight undertone of bitterness from the cocoa-rich chocolate. Perfect. I dollop the chocolaty mix into six small ramekin dishes and put them into my preheated oven to cook for ten minutes.

Now all three dishes are in the oven. Success! These three recipes are definitely going to go in *The Amelie Day Book of Baking*. I'm confident that I have them down to a fine art.

Before I steady myself on the counter, I pull the macaroons out of the oven and let them cool. My head is damp with sweat, and my chest feels terrible, but it's like I'm on another planet where nothing matters except the moment I'm in. I'm not even really aware of the other contestants, even though I can hear slamming oven doors, clanking pans, and the hiss of steam coming from all directions. The lights are so bright that I can't see anybody anyway.

I need to take my mini lava cakes out. I don't know whether the runny center worked, but they look like they've risen, and the deep dark-chocolate smell makes my taste buds zing into action. I put the cakes onto white plates, and then I whisk some vanilla and powdered sugar into heavy cream to make the Chantilly crème to serve with them. When that's done, I pour the cream into six tiny glasses to be put on each plate.

Then I add milk and cream into a saucepan for my vanilla custard and slice open a black vanilla pod with the tip of a sharp knife. My hands are shaking so much that I have to be careful not to slice off my fingers. I scrape the seeds from the pod onto the tip of my knife and then slide them into the mixture, bring it to a boil, and put the eggs and sugar into another bowl. I mix them together, pour in the milk mixture, and whisk it all together before transferring it back into the pan.

Then I leave the whole thing to cook for fifteen minutes, stirring almost the whole time until it is dense enough to coat the back of my spoon with thick, sweet, yellow custard. While it's bubbling, I trim the rice paper around my macaroons so that it fits in a neat circle under each cookie.

I'm boiling now. My face is dripping sweat, and I feel dizzy, but all I can focus on is the food.

I wipe down all my surfaces to remove the mess of flour and butter and powdered sugar. Then, while the custard is cooking, I take my German gingerbread out of the oven and brush the top with butter.

It looks amazing. The cake is hot and soft. I slice it and inhale the hot, gingery steam but not enough to risk making myself cough — just a tiny sniff. Then I put a couple of slices on a white plate, and I pour my thick yellow vanilla custard from the saucepan into a tiny white creamer and put this next to it. I dust the white powdered sugar over the top of the cake as a contrast, even though I didn't rehearse it this way. It looks like fresh snow on dark earth. That's what I like best about cooking. You can make stuff up as you go.

I stand back and wipe my forehead with my sleeve.

And just in time.

"STOP COOKING!" yells the bald guy.

That's it. The two hours are up. They went so fast I hardly had time to breathe, which is not good when you have CF, since breathing is difficult even on a good day.

I glance around. Two of the other contestants are frantically trying to finish plating their dishes.

I wash my hands, wipe the edges of my three plates of food with a dish towel so that there are no messy smudges, and arrange them on the work surface in front of me, ready for judging.

Then I try to calm my beating heart, which is difficult when you have CF, because the usual way of taking deep, steadying breaths is not really an option.

The presenter starts to make his way around with the judges to all twelve of the contestants. I'm about sixth in line to be interviewed, so I have time to stand and catch my breath and steady myself against the granite counter before they get to me.

Then there's a commotion behind the camera.

I try not to look, because we're supposed to be standing calm and collected behind our workstations and not gawking at the camera, but I can't help it.

The lights in here are very bright. All I can see is a pair of arms waving in the air as if in the middle of an argument, and then Elaine, the floor manager, comes up just behind the camera so she can't be seen on TV, and she gestures to me to come off the set.

I look left and right just in case she is gesturing to one of the other contestants, but she's definitely pointing at me.

My heart sinks. I step down from the workstation and leave all my lovely gleaming pots and pans behind. My three dishes sit ready for the judges, and they look really good. Why am I being called off the set? I don't look *that* sick, do I? I thought Chell did a pretty good job on my makeup.

Then I'm hustled behind the cameras and out of the studio into a little room.

A woman leaps up and comes toward me with a pale face and her arms outstretched.

"Mom!" I say. "What are you doing here?"

Then another figure comes out from behind her.

It's my father. And he reaches out to hug me, too.

I'm more scared than I've ever been in my life.

There's something terribly wrong with their faces.

For one thing, they're not angry.

My mother holds onto me so tight that I start to suffocate and have to pull my face out of her soft cashmere top.

"Oh, Amelie," she says. "Sit down. We need to talk to you. In private."

CHAPTER 15

I sit down with my parents, one on either side of me. They each take one of my hands.

"Stop it," I say. "You're scaring me! Why aren't you angry? Harry said you were angry!"

Mom glances at Dad. She's trying not to cry. "We have to tell you something," she says. "Don't worry. It'll be all right." She gets up and goes to stare out the window at the busy street outside.

"How did you get here so fast?" I ask them.

"We drove," Dad says. "We wanted to get here as quickly as we could."

I look at Mom. She looks in one piece, despite the fact that she's crying into a tissue.

"Who — what?" I say, confused. "Why isn't Harry here? He should have been here forever ago. He was coming to get me. Why — oh, no. Please don't tell me that. PLEASE DON'T TELL ME."

I start to shake. I stare at my parents, wide-eyed. Why aren't they speaking? Shouldn't they be reassuring me that Harry is fine, that he's outside in the car waiting for us, or at home waiting for me to come back from New York?

Somehow, my parents don't need to speak. Their eyes and ashen faces are telling me everything I really don't want to know.

"What happened?" I say. I feel like I need to hold it together somehow, or I'm going to start yelling and screaming and never stop.

"He was rushing to catch a train," says Dad. "He stepped out onto Market Street without looking, from what we can gather. The van was going too fast, couldn't stop in time. He's in the West Clinton hospital."

I stare at Dad, not understanding. "Do you mean . . . he's not . . . you know?" I say. I can't bring myself to say the word in case saying it makes it happen. A vision of Harry's curly dark brown hair and brown eyes flashes in front of my eyes. I've always liked the freckles across the bridge of his nose and the way that his eyes seem to get darker when he's serious about something.

We all have to die sometime, right? Any of us could die tomorrow.

The tears are flowing now. Mom comes over and gives me a tissue. Then she holds a bowl underneath my mouth while I almost cough myself unconscious.

"He's in critical condition," she says. "His parents are at his bedside. That's why we came to get you. We need to get there as soon as possible, but I have to warn you, Amelie. We might not make it in time."

I get up. "What are we waiting for?" I say. "I have to see Harry. I have to."

Then we leave the TV studio without ever looking back.

***

In the car, Mom sits in the back while Dad drives and I sit up front.

She passes me an inhaler and a nebulizer and tells me to use them. Then she hooks me up to an oxygen tank, and I take deep, steadying breaths until at last the tightness in my chest calms down a little and my breath comes more easily.

Then she forces me to eat a sandwich and some Creon followed by a protein shake and a bar of chocolate. I feel like eating is the last thing I ever want to do, but I know that there's no point arguing. It's such a relief to have my meds again and to finally feel like I'm not about to pass out.

I lean back against the seat and close my eyes for the entire ride back. I'm not asleep, but I'm thinking about all the good things that Harry has done for me since we were little, and I'm replaying them over and over while silent tears pour down my cheeks.

When we pull up to the hospital, I sit up. My heart starts to pound, and I feel shaky.

"You'll come in with me, right?" I ask Mom. "Even though you're probably really angry with me."

Mom sighs and wipes the tears from my cheeks with her tissue. "Well, I was," she says. "But then I was so relieved to know where you were. You should never have done this, Amelie. You should never have traveled to New York in the state that you were in. You should never have run off when you were supposed to be in the hospital for an operation. And you should *never* have lied to me and your father and poor Harry the way you did."

She does still sound a little angry underneath the weariness. I wish she hadn't said that last part. But the thing is, it's true.

If I hadn't lied and gone to New York, Harry wouldn't have tried to rush after me. He would still be at school playing football or leaping around on the tennis courts.

If anything happens to him . . . if anything happens to Harry, it's all my fault. I'll never forgive myself. Never.

The three of us walk into the hospital in silence.

***

Harry's parents are sitting one on either side of his bed as we come in.

Mom and Dad go straight to them and offer hugs of sympathy. Our parents have been friends for many years.

I try not to look at Harry. There's a mass of tubes and machines all over him.

"Hello, Mel," says Harry's father. He's always been kind to me, ever since I was a little girl and they lived next door. I like his gray hair and black glasses and the way he's holding Harry's hand. "Come sit by the bed."

I look at his mother. She's staring at me, but the expression on her face is hard to read. Except that I can read it, or at least I think I can. It says: *You've got a lot of nerve, turning up here. If it weren't for your stupid, selfish trip to New York, my son would still be at home doing his homework or out playing football. You don't deserve to be here at his bedside. I wish you hadn't come.*

I stare at my feet.

"Come on," says Harry's father, holding his hand out to me. "It's okay."

I look at Mom and Dad behind me, and they nod and then back into the hallway. There aren't supposed to be more than two visitors at a time, but that still leaves three of us in the room.

"I'll go and get some coffee," says Harry's mom. She stands up and stretches her back with a grimace. Her face is streaked with tears and makeup. "Let me know right away if anything changes, Adam."

She walks past me, taking care not to brush against me. Probably a good thing. I feel so feeble that I'd probably fall to the floor. Mom says that I need to go to the CF center on the way home and get checked out. She thinks that I have another chest infection, and she might be right. We haven't yet touched on the sensitive subject of the operation I was supposed to be having this morning.

Harry's dad gestures at the empty chair next to the bed.

I creep over to it, feeling awkward and shaken to the core. I can't not look at Harry with his dad right here, so I turn and look down at his face. Most of it is obscured by tubes in his mouth, tubes up his nose, and a large bandage right around the top of his head. His eyes are shut, and what I can see of his face is bruised and cut and bloody.

It's all wrong, seeing big, healthy, red-cheeked Harry in a hospital bed. Somebody might as well have picked up a bucket of dirt and thrown it on the soft white pillows.

"He looks like he's asleep," I say and then I regret it right away. I'm such an idiot. If he was asleep, he wouldn't be covered in all this medical stuff now, would he?

"Well, he kind of is," says Harry's father. His voice is shaking a little, and I can tell he's being careful to keep his voice measured and kind. "Unfortunately, he's in a coma. That's a little more serious."

I blush and nod.

"You can hold his hand if you want," says Harry's dad. "And you can talk to him. You never know, he might be able to hear it somehow."

I take Harry's limp hand in my own. It's cool and soft. Then I clear my throat and prepare to say something, but it's really embarrassing with Harry's father sitting on the other side of the bed.

As if he senses this, Harry's dad gets up and smiles at me. Then he heads outside, and I see him put his arm around Harry's mother and persuade her to stay in the hall for a little longer.

I wait until the door has closed, and then I put Harry's hand up to my cheek and hold it there in silence for a moment.

You know when you just kind of assume that somebody is going to be in your life forever? Well, I thought that Harry and I would be going out for the rest of our lives and that one day, we might even get married. When we stopped being little friends who played soccer together and he asked me out, my mother gave me the CF Police lecture about how I shouldn't get too hung up on my first-ever boyfriend, because first loves never last, and I should put my health first and all that stuff. Then when we'd been going out for three months and then six months, my parents decided to accept it.

Harry is part of the fabric of my life.

And he gets my CF. He never makes me feel bad about it or inadequate, and although he kind of nags me about my medication, it's only because he cares about me so much.

Part of me wishes I'd told Harry I was going to New York in the first place, but if I had, I'm sure he would have tried to stop me.

It all seems kind of stupid now, my obsession with baking.

I put a bunch of cake, eggs, and butter ahead of my own boyfriend and my family, and I lied to them and worried them and left them behind just so I could enter a stupid competition.

"I'm sorry, Harry," I whisper into his cold hand. "I'm

so, so sorry. I'm the worst girlfriend in the universe, and I completely understand if you want to dump me the moment you wake up."

That's if he does wake up. The doctors told Mom that it's likely he'll never regain consciousness and that his parents might have to make the heartbreaking decision to turn off his life-support machine.

I'm trying not to think about that option.

This is Harry. *My* Harry. My big, cheerful, red-cheeked, floppy-haired Harry.

He's not going anywhere while I've got a say in the matter.

"I have to go," I whisper. Harry's mom is hovering outside the door, looking anguished. "Your mom's coming to sit with you now. But I'll be back tomorrow."

I give him a peck on the forehead and go outside to where my parents are sitting in the hall on plastic orange chairs.

They spring up when I come out.

"I know it's not easy for you, sweetheart," says Mom. She puts her arms around me. "But we need to go and get you checked out now. The last thing we all need is you getting sicker again."

I bury my head in her chest and sob dry, painful sobs mixed with retching coughs. Dad rubs my back in silence. These have been the worst two days of my life, aside from that part when I baked my recipes for the competition. That part felt good.

But that's not real life. Real life is Mom, Dad, Harry, and me.

And CF.

***

Turns out I'm actually really sick.

Dr. Rogers is on vacation, so I see another physician at the CF center, and as soon as she's examined me and listened to my cough, she tells Mom that to be safe, they're going to admit me until this infection clears.

I try to protest, but I've got a fever and I'm all shivery and super-tired so I don't argue much. It's kind of a relief to be tucked up in the soft white hospital bed. I have antibiotics being pumped into my system, and I'm really dehydrated after New York, so I'm hooked up to a fluid drip, too.

The thing I hate most about it is that I'm not allowed out of bed to go see Harry.

***

On the third day, I have an operation to put the gastrostomy in my stomach.

I have to be put to sleep for it, so when I wake up, I'm groggy and kind of sore, but the first thing I ask Mom is if there is any news about Harry, and she shakes her head.

"No change," she says. "Sorry. I know that's not what you want to hear."

I lie back on the thick hospital pillows and let the tears trickle down my face with my eyes closed. Mom sits next to me and holds my hand until I go to sleep.

The next time I wake up, Dad is sitting by the bed.

"What day is it?" I ask, confused. The blinds in the room are drawn so I can't tell.

"Same day you had your operation," says Dad. "Evening. They said you can go home tomorrow, Mel. That's great news, isn't it?"

I smile, because it's what he wants me to do, but underneath I feel sad and hollow. I can't imagine what going home and not being with Harry is going to feel like. All I can see stretching out ahead of me is grief and loneliness and the continuing burden of my CF as it gets worse and worse.

"I feel awful," I say to Dad.

He nods. "Soon your mom will have you feeling good as new," he says. "Oh, and she's got some news for you. I'll let her tell you herself."

I prop myself up into a sitting position with a grimace. I've got a small scar where the gastrostomy and the button that closes it off are, and it tugs and pulls when I bend.

Mom comes in smiling with a bunch of yellow daffodils. She arranges them in the vase by my bed and then sits beside me, her eyes twinkling.

"What?" I say. "Is it Harry? Did he wake up?"

Mom chews her lip. "Oh, sorry, no," she says. "I wish I could tell you that. But it's something you might want to hear anyway."

"Are you and Dad getting back together?" I ask. That would be weird, but good.

"Oh, sorry, no," says Mom again. "We're getting along fine, which is a good reason not to live with one another again."

"Well, what then?" I ask. This is turning into a tiring question-and-answer game.

Then she tells me.

She's heard from the network that produces *Best Teen Baker*. They said that the judges were so impressed with the three dishes I left behind when I rushed off that they approved me to move on to the semifinals.

"They said that you managed to pull off the perfect lava cake," says Mom. "They said that when they cut into it, you could hear gasps of delight from the judges as the chocolate oozed out of the middle!"

She's nearly bouncing up and down on the bed. My wound feels hot and sore. I give her a pained look and have to put out a hand to stop her.

"Oh," I say cautiously. "But haven't I missed the filming for the semifinals?"

"Nope," Mom says smugly. "They said that they'll postpone it until you're healthy enough to travel. And this time I can come with you."

I force a small smile, but my insides are aching with love and pain for Harry, so it's difficult to look too excited.

"I can't go," I say to her. "How can I leave Harry? I just can't go."

Mom's smile fades, but then she nods and takes my hand. "Never mind, honey," she says. "It's great to be praised by the judges that way. You should be proud."

We talk some more about the competition for a while, but underneath I feel anything but proud.

I made my sweet, kind boyfriend rush up to New York City to rescue me, and then he got run over.

How can I ever feel proud of myself again?

CHAPTER 16

When I get out of the hospital, I rest at home for a couple of days.

Trish comes to the house and shows Mom and me how to hook a tube to my gastrostomy so that I can get extra calories while I'm asleep. At first I can't sleep because I swear I can feel the liquid going into me. The tube always has to be switched off at four in the morning and flushed through and disconnected, and the tubes from the oxygen tank feel uncomfortable as well, so I guess that's it for ever getting a decent night's sleep again. But I get used to the gastrostomy pretty quickly, so I don't feel quite as depressed. Even after just two days, I weigh a little more, so I'm happy about that, and so is Mom, but this horrible sadness drags me down every waking moment of the day.

I go back to school, and Jenna makes sure that I don't get overtired, and she tells anybody who says anything nasty about me to back off, and for once they do. Everybody knows about Harry. He is one of the most popular boys in his grade, so I get a good amount of people coming up to me and asking how he's doing.

I always tell them the same thing: "He's alive, which is the important thing."

But he hasn't come out of the coma.

I go outside every lunch break and sit with Jenna under the old oak tree where I used to sit with Harry, and sometimes we chat and other times I'm silent and don't feel much like talking, and she's fine with that.

I feel guilty for having been resentful of Jenna's health. She's a good friend — the best. And she's always there for me. So I tell her how I'm feeling, and she nods and holds my hand.

***

I'm back working in Karim's store.

He's agreed to start paying me in money. Now every time I think about baking (which, let's face it, used to be pretty much 24/7), I feel a big pang of sadness and anxiety in the pit of my stomach, and I picture Harry's pale face on the hospital pillow, and I know that it's all my fault he's there.

So I stop baking.

I stop reading cookbooks and watching cooking shows. I empty all my ingredients out of the cupboards at home and throw a lot of it away.

Mom watches me with a sad look in her eye but doesn't dare speak. I'm on a short fuse from all the worrying about Harry and the plunge my own health has taken.

I no longer fill my cart with flour, eggs, and sugar at Karim's shop. Karim is paying me now, even though I'm still thirteen and it's still not technically legal for me to work here. I think he feels sorry for me. He counts out the bills at the end of the day and puts them in my hand with a sad look in his eyes.

"It's no good — Little Girl Who Bakes not baking," he says. "No good at all."

"You're just saying that because it costs you more to pay me money," I say with a sad smile, but he's not having any of it and goes back to the cash, still shaking his head and making a noise that sounds like "I, I, I." I pocket the money and head home. I'm not sure what I'm going to do with my pay yet. Maybe I'll go shopping with Jenna more often.

When I get home after my third day back at the grocery store, Mom's right there the second I open the front door.

"The hospital called," she says, out of breath. She shoves a coat in my direction and grabs her keys from the hall table. "We have to go there. Now."

Mom won't say anything on the way. She drives fast, and I swear she ran a few red lights, but she just mutters a rude word, makes a face, and continues at the same speed.

"He's not — he's not . . ." I say, unable to get the words out. I look at Mom's face. She doesn't look like anybody has died. Then again, it's sometimes hard to tell with Mom.

"Oh — no," she says. "Sorry. I didn't mean to worry you."

We pull into the hospital parking lot, and Mom grabs my hand and almost pulls me at a run toward the entrance, and then she remembers that I find it kind of hard to breathe and that I was just released from the hospital myself, so she slows down to a power walk.

I'm still panting and coughing by the time we get up to the fourth floor.

Mom propels me past a smiling nurse and a smiling doctor in a white coat. Another smiling nurse comes out of Harry's room and almost claps her hands when she sees me. Everybody seems to be moving in slow motion for some reason. I have time to notice the gold filling in her front tooth when she smiles and read the white name badge with black lettering on her blue uniform.

Harry's parents leap up when they see me come in. They're both smiling, too. His mother looks about twenty years younger and really pretty. "Oh, Amelie," she says. "He woke up! Quick — come and see."

I'm already in tears.

Harry's dad vacates his chair for me, and I sit down and find myself staring straight into Harry's deep brown eyes.

"Hi," I croak. I turn away and cough for a moment. Mom offers a bowl, but I shake my head and turn back to Harry. He blinks at me, and a slow smile spreads across his face. He's still wired up to machines and tubes, but this time his grip on my hand is strong and warm.

"He won't be able to say much," warns his mother. "But he's back with us. That's what counts."

She blows her nose and rests her cheek on Harry's dad's shoulder. I can hear my own mother sniffling behind me.

"Cup . . ." says Harry, or at least something that sounds like that. "Cup . . ."

He reaches up with his right hand and removes the oxygen mask from his face.

I frown and lean down so that my head is near his mouth. "Try it again," I say. "I'm listening."

Harry summons all his strength. "Cupcakes," he says.

"What did he say?" says his mom. "I swear he just said 'cupcakes!' But that can't be right."

I laugh through my tears. "Yeah, it is," I say. "My chocolate cupcakes. They're kind of his favorite."

"Oh," says his mother, relaxing. "That's a relief. For a moment there I thought he'd lost his mind in the accident."

A while later, they go out and leave me alone with Harry. He goes to sleep, but it's kind of nice listening to him breathe and knowing that he's going to wake up again. The doctors say that his recovery is going to take a long, long time and that he might have to learn how to walk all over again, but at least he's heading in the right direction now.

***

On the way home, I'm quiet, mulling it all over.

"I might do that competition after all," I say from the

passenger's seat, where I'm eating some peanut butter M&M's and a bag of potato chips. "I think Harry would want me to do it."

"You're right about that," says Mom. "But I'm coming with you this time, Amelie. No more running away to New York City and giving me a heart attack."

I turn to look at my mom. I see her tired face and the lines underneath her eyes that have come from worrying about and caring for me every single day of my CF life. I realize something else, too. She's scared. One day she's going to have to face losing me for good, and she's scared.

"I'm really sorry, Mom," I say. "I shouldn't have put my own stupid obsession ahead of you. I promise I won't let it happen again."

Mom laughs. "You're a teenager!" she says. "Of course it will happen again."

***

When I get home, I log in to my blog for the first time in a while.

Tons of people have heard about what I was planning to do and have written to wish me good luck in the competition. Part of me wants to give a spoon-by-spoon account of the competition and what I cooked and how it turned out, but that seems kind of insensitive given that my boyfriend is in the hospital and that my parents are going to have to learn to trust me all over again. So instead I write a short paragraph explaining that I went to the competition in New York City, but my boyfriend was in an accident. Then I write this:

Thanks for all your nice posts and recipes. There seem to be a bunch of big hurdles ahead of me. I have tons of schoolwork to catch up on and tests to study for. Anyway, it's going to take a very long time for Harry to get better. The doctors say that he will be in a wheelchair, and he'll have to miss a lot of school. I think he'll be really upset now that he can't play sports. He has spent years being my support system, and now I'm going to have to learn to be his. It seems kind of ironic that he's sick now, too, and I'll have to take care of him. I get the feeling that this is going to take a lot more than just a batch of cupcakes. And behind all this is the threat of my lung transplant. I could be waiting for years, or I could get a call any day now. Nobody really knows. And even if I did get new lungs, the doctors warned me that my body might reject them, and then I'd be back to square one. And while I'm waiting to get the new lungs, I could go downhill fast and end up in the hospital for good. I might even die if my lung function drops any further.

I screw up my face against all these scary thoughts. I wish for about the millionth time that I could just be a normal teenager worrying about tests and zits and boys. I don't know how I could cope with life if I'd really removed my great passion of baking from it. I've just realized that apart from Harry, baking is the only thing that really helps me cope with my CF. It was probably a little hasty to throw out all my ingredients. A future without Flour Power looks bleak and boring and kind of . . . uncooked.

I look back at the computer screen and type some more.

But maybe I need to bake myself through *Best Teen Baker* if I want to achieve my life's ambition of getting to the final and maybe even winning. After all, I live to bake. If I stop baking, I might stop living. And please, keep sending your recipes. I might ask to borrow them for my best-selling book of the future, *The Amelie Day Book of Baking.*

I snap the computer shut.

A vision of Harry floats in front of my eyes.

"Mom," I say, going downstairs. "Can you give me a ride to Karim's shop?"

Mom's reading the newspaper downstairs. She takes off her glasses and rubs her eyes. Her skin looks dry and tired, and her eyes are like slits from lack of sleep. "What do you want to buy?" she asks. "We have tons of food in the kitchen."

I roll my eyes and give her an impatient smile. "I have to make Harry's cupcakes," I say. "I need chocolate, eggs, flour, and butter, like *now*."

My mother's face lights up and sparkles in the late afternoon sun. She grabs the car keys and we head outside.

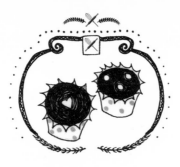

Harry's Favorite
Chocolate Heart Cupcakes

To make 12 of these gorgeous chocolaty treats, you will need:

- 1 ½ cups flour
- 1 cup granulated sugar
- 1 ¼ cup cocoa powder
- 1 stick butter
- 2 eggs
- ¼ cup evaporated milk or whole milk
- ¼ cup water

To decorate:

- A large bar of milk chocolate or store-bought frosting
- A small ball of fondant icing and red food coloring, or Hershey's Kisses, sprinkles, gumdrops, or M&M's

Preheat the oven to 350°F.

Put 12 cupcake liners into the muffin tin and set aside for later.

Cream the butter and sugar together in a bowl with a wooden spoon. Then beat in the eggs, one at a time. Sieve the flour, then add it to the mix and beat in until smooth. Then add your cocoa powder. Add ¼ cup of whole milk (if you like your cakes light and springy) or instead, you could use ¼ cup of evaporated milk (this gives a much creamier, moister texture). Finally, add ¼ cup of water and beat the mixture until you have a nice smooth mix.

Spoon the mixture into your prepared muffin tin so that each cupcake liner is about three-quarters full. Slide the pan into your oven and bake for about 20 minutes or until firm.

You can ice the cupcakes with frosting, or you can do what I like best — melt a large bar of milk chocolate, then brush the chocolate all over the top of each little cupcake.

Harry is picky about cupcakes. I once put a red fondant heart on one of his and ever since then, he expects it. If you want to make a heart, too, you can add some drops of red food coloring to a small ball of fondant. Roll it in your hands until the dough turns pinkish, roll it out with a rolling pin, and then use a tiny heart-shaped cookie cutter to cut out a heart. But be warned, your hands will look like something out of a horror film afterward.

Or a much easier way to top off the milk chocolate on your cupcakes is to buy some candy and stick some on top of each cake. You can use chocolate sprinkles, or M&M's, or almost anything you want.

After they've cooled down, these need to be kept in an airtight container. But in our house, they never last that long!

Glossary

antibiotic (an-ti-bye-OT-ik) — a drug used to kill bacteria and cure infections

autogenic drainage (aw-toh-JEN-ik DREY-nij) — a type of breathing exercise that can be done without equipment and helps remove mucus from airways

cystic fibrosis (SIS-tik fye-BRO-sis) — an inherited, life-threatening disorder that causes critical damage to the lungs and digestive system

enzyme (EN-zime) — a type of protein in humans, animals, and plants that causes chemical reactions to occur, like breaking food down so it can be digested

gastrostomy (ga-STROS-tuh-mee) — an opening that's created through surgery and leads to the stomach; the opening is usually used for feeding

morbid (MOR-bid) — relating to death

nebulizer (NEB-yuh-lye-zur) — a device that makes a liquid drug into a mist so that it can be inhaled

port (POHRT) — a small medical device put in just below the skin that allows for a person to easily inject medicine or take blood samples

sponge (SPUHNJ) — the bread-like part of a cake, usually made with a base of yeast, liquid, and flour

THE FUN DOESN'T STOP HERE!

Expanded backmatter, including writing prompts and discussion questions, is available at

WWW.CAPSTONEPUB.COM

Find cool websites and more books like this one at **WWW.FACTHOUND.COM**. Just type in the BOOK ID: 9781496522160 and you're ready to go!

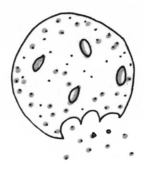

Author's Note

The Baking Life of Amelie Day is a work of fiction based on my own particular research. It is important to note that cystic fibrosis (CF) affects different people in different ways. I wrote this book after watching a television documentary about CF. It followed a group of young people who were waiting for life-saving lung transplants, and I was touched by the daily struggles they had just to stay alive. Cystic fibrosis is a life-shortening genetic condition that slowly destroys the lungs and digestive system, and there's currently no cure. Only half of sufferers live to celebrate their fortieth birthday. To find out more about cystic fibrosis, you can contact the Cystic Fibrosis Foundation at www.cff.org. You may also want to follow the blog of Victoria Tremlett, who lives with CF, at www.tor-pastthepointofnoreturn.blogspot.co.uk. Some of my research was aided by Oliver Jackson, who lives with CF, and I'd like to thank him for his input.

About the Author

Vanessa Curtis is the award-winning author of several young adult novels including *Zelah Green* (Egmont, 2009), which won the Manchester Children's Book Prize and was shortlisted for the 2009 Waterstones Prize, and *The Haunting of Tabitha Gray* (Egmont, 2012), a contemporary ghost story with a shocking twist.